SOPHIE BROOKS MYSTERIES

DAISY LANDISH

BEACHES AND TRAILS
PUBLISHING

CHAPTER 1
HARVEST OF BEGINNINGS

THE WINDING ROADS of Sonoma unfurled before Sophie Brooks, her car rumbling along as she maneuvered through the heart of California's wine country. Even with the early January chill, the landscape stretched lush and vibrant, rows of grapevines sprawling in perfect lines under a cloudy sky. Her destination—a quaint guesthouse on the edge of Cartwright Vineyard—came into view, sparking a flicker of anticipation she hadn't felt in months.

She parked and took in the cottage before her: a small, rustic structure with ivy crawling up the sides, warm light spilling from its windows, and the soft scent of earth and grapes mingling in the air. It was the perfect hideaway, peaceful and tucked away from the world—or, more importantly, far from her old life.

Sophie stepped out, the gravel crunching under her boots. This was it. Her new beginning. After the heartbreak and upheaval of the past year, she was here to rebuild, rediscover, and hopefully, rejuvenate herself. Sonoma was her refuge—a place to lose herself in the art of food, to pour her passion into her blog and her book, and to leave behind the lingering ache Oregon had left in her heart.

Inside the cottage, the faint aroma of cedar and lemon greeted her. The decor was rustic but inviting—weathered wood floors, a cozy armchair by the window, and a small kitchen that practically invited her to cook. Running her fingers along the countertop, she imagined all the dishes she'd create here, the flavors she'd uncover in this little pocket of wine country.

Sighing, she set her bags down and looked around. The space was her own, yet strangely unfamiliar, and a pang of loneliness crept in, uninvited. She pushed the feeling away. Sonoma was about healing, about starting fresh. She was done looking back. She had work to do.

Taking a steadying breath, she allowed herself a small smile as she glanced around the cottage. It was liberating, knowing that every choice here was hers. No compromises, no half-truths, just her instincts. The contrast with her Oregon life felt jarring. She recalled all the times Ryan had brushed off her opinions with a dismissive, "Don't worry, I've got it covered," as though her thoughts were... less.

This chance in Sonoma felt vital. It wasn't only about escaping betrayal but about learning to rely on herself completely—to trust her own intuition. This time, she alone would make the choices, solve the mysteries, and define her future. The thought filled her with a rare satisfaction.

She glanced around the cozy room, feeling a sense of belonging slowly settle within her. Here, each decision, each moment, added a new layer to her story, independent of anyone else's expectations. For the first time in ages, Sophie was exactly where she wanted to be.

Sophie pulled out her phone and opened the app for her blog, her fingers itching to start her first Sonoma post. But instead of typing, she stared at the screen, memories washing over her—the bustling restaurant she'd left behind, shared dreams with Ryan, the way he'd betrayed all of it. She remembered that awful night when she'd discovered his under-the-table dealings, how he'd compromised everything they'd built together.

Enough, she told herself, tucking the phone away. This was her new chapter—no filters, no second-guessing. It felt like an act of defiance, a promise to herself to be fully present in the life she was creating.

Deciding to head into town to clear her mind, Sophie shrugged on her coat and stepped outside. The air was cool and crisp, carrying the scent of damp soil, oak, and a faint hint of rosemary from the wild shrubs bordering the vineyard. Each breath felt cleansing, rooting her in the present moment.

The town square wasn't far—a charming cluster of boutique shops, cafes, and markets surrounding an old stone fountain. Holiday lights still adorned the streets, their gentle glow reflecting off shop windows, lending the town an inviting warmth. She felt welcomed, like this little square had been waiting for her.

Sophie took her time browsing the local produce at the farmer's market, her fingers grazing over crisp apples, leafy greens, and handmade cheeses. This was the kind of place she'd dreamed of back in her hurried restaurant days, where each ingredient told its own story, untouched by the urgency and shortcuts she'd known. Here, people lived by the rhythms of the earth—a world away from Oregon's frenetic kitchen life. Sonoma didn't rush her; it let her breathe, giving her space to heal.

As she picked up a bunch of rosemary, a warm, friendly voice sounded beside her. "I see you're already drawn to our finest herbs."

Sophie turned to see a woman about her age, with shoulder-length, chestnut hair and a friendly smile. She wore a worn, flannel shirt over jeans, her eyes lively with curiosity.

"I guess I can't resist," Sophie replied, smiling. "It's a force of habit."

"Welcome to the club. I'm Claire Cartwright," the woman said, extending a hand. "You're new in town, aren't you?"

Sophie nodded, returning the handshake. "Sophie Brooks. Just arrived today, actually. I'll be here for a few months, staying at the guesthouse near Cartwright Vineyard."

"Ah, you're right next door to us," Claire said, her face lighting up. "My uncle James owns the vineyard. It's been in our family for decades. Let me know if you'd like a tour sometime."

Sophie's interest piqued. "I'd love that. I'm a food blogger, so I'm always looking for good stories, especially those tied to local ingredients."

"Well, you've come to the right place," Claire said with a grin. "Sonoma takes its farm-to-table tradition very seriously. Though I should warn you, it's not all as peaceful as it looks."

"Oh?" Sophie tilted her head, intrigued.

Claire hesitated, glancing toward the vineyard. "It's

probably nothing," she said with a shrug. "Just a bit of family drama—old vineyard rivalries and all that."

Sophie sensed there was more to the story, but before she could ask, her phone buzzed. A message from Oliver lit up the screen.

> Oliver: Update, please! How's my favorite detective doing in wine country? 🍇 🕵️

Sophie chuckled and typed back a quick response.

> Sophie: Just met my first new friend! I think Sonoma will be... interesting.

> Oliver: You got this! Sip some wine, sniff some grapes, and don't let your detective instincts go to waste. 🍷

She tucked her phone away, feeling reassured by his words. Claire continued chatting, sharing local tips and pointing out nearby cafes and shops Sophie might enjoy. Soon, Sophie genuinely looked forward to the months ahead, the weight of her past loosening its grip.

As the sun set, casting a golden glow over the vineyards, Sophie returned to the guesthouse. She opened her laptop this time, intending to start her first Sonoma post, wanting her readers to feel the quiet beauty of this place and the slow, earthy rhythm that already felt like a balm.

She titled her draft, A New Beginning: Sonoma's Secrets and Stories, and let her fingers flow over the keys:

There's a kind of peace here that you don't find in many places—a stillness that lets you breathe. Sonoma is a world all its own. The grapevines have seen more years than I can count, and every corner seems to hold a story. While I'm here, I hope to discover a few of them.

Sophie paused, a faint smile on her lips. This was exactly where she needed to be. Saving her draft, a quiet satisfaction settled over her, replacing the hollow ache she'd carried for too long. Here, surrounded by unfamiliar faces and places, Sophie felt the first glimmer of hope.

Tonight, she would let herself settle into that feeling. Tomorrow, the mystery of Sonoma awaited her.

CHAPTER 2
MARKET BOUNTY

SOPHIE WOKE to the muted sound of birdsong outside her window and the scent of damp earth and grapevines drifting into the cottage. Sonoma mornings were unlike any she'd known—a slow unfolding, without the rush and noise that had filled her days in Oregon. Here, time felt different, stretched and softened by the vineyards and hills. She let herself sink into the stillness, her heartbeat steadying, as if the land itself offered a quiet kind of healing.

Morning light filtered through the thin curtains, casting a soft glow over the rustic furnishings. The space felt both familiar and foreign, as though it were still adjusting to the fragments of her life she'd brought with her.

After a quick breakfast of tea and toast, Sophie packed her camera and notebook, deciding to take Claire up on her offer of a vineyard tour. Outside, the air was fresh and crisp, carrying hints of damp earth and crushed leaves. As she stepped out, she felt the weight of old worries lift, replaced by a quiet sense of possibility. There was no clamor here, no rush—just the steady rhythm of the vines breathing around her. She let her fingers brush against the sturdy grape leaves, drawing in their subtle, earthy aroma. It felt like Sonoma's soil was rooting her back to herself.

Approaching Cartwright Vineyard, she noticed Claire waving from under a large oak tree by the entrance. Sophie quickened her step, smiling at the sight of her first new friend in Sonoma.

"Ready for a taste of vineyard life?" Claire greeted her with a grin.

"I can't wait," Sophie replied, genuinely looking forward to the experience. "I've always loved knowing the story behind the ingredients I use."

Claire's face lit up as they began walking through the rows of grapevines. "You'll get plenty of stories here," she said, gesturing to the neat rows of vines rolling over the hills. "Our family's been on this land for three generations. My uncle James works hard to keep the vineyard sustainable. He's big on quality and tradition."

Sophie noted the pride in Claire's voice. "It must feel amazing to be part of something with such history." She reached out to touch a budding vine, feeling its delicate strength. In some ways, she felt like this vineyard was a mirror—new shoots emerging from roots that had weathered storms. "These vines," she murmured, "they come back every year, don't they? No matter what happens."

Claire nodded, and Sophie smiled. There was something hopeful in that—a reminder of her own resilience and potential for regrowth.

"It is," Claire agreed, though her smile faltered briefly. She recovered quickly, but Sophie caught the shadow of something unspoken, filing it away. Maybe the "family drama" Claire had mentioned ran deeper than she'd let on.

"Over there's the main barn," Claire said, pointing toward a large, wooden structure where workers were loading crates. "We host tastings and small events there during the harvest. The stone building beyond is the fermentation cellar, where all the magic happens."

As they neared the fermentation cellar, Claire paused, her expression darkening. She bit her lip, glancing back over her shoulder as if to check for onlookers.

"Actually, Sophie… something happened yesterday," Claire murmured, her voice low. "I didn't want to worry you, especially since you're new, but I think you should know."

Sophie's curiosity sharpened. "What happened?"

"One of our main irrigation lines was damaged—deliberately. Water gushed everywhere, soaking the roots of some of our best vines before we stopped it." Claire's gaze hardened. "It had to be deliberate. Nothing in our equipment could accidentally cut through pipes like that."

Sophie felt a chill. "Do you have any idea who might have done it?"

Claire shook her head. "Not exactly. But… let's just say this kind of thing has happened before. A few years back, one of the smaller vineyards had a fire in their tasting room. Suspicious, but the investigation went nowhere. My uncle thinks Angela's influence stretches further than people realize. She owns the vineyard to the west."

Sophie absorbed Claire's words, her pulse quickening. This wasn't just rivalry. It was calculated sabotage. Damage like this would hit James where it hurt the most, making it hard to keep up with production and tempting him to sell.

"Has James gone to the authorities?" Sophie asked, keeping her voice low.

Claire looked down, frustration tightening her expression. "He tried, after another incident last year. But without proof—and with Angela's friends on the town council—there's not much they're willing to do. They wrote it off as an accident." She looked back up, her eyes fierce. "But, I know it wasn't. And now, with this latest attack, I can't shake the feeling they're trying to wear him down, to force him out."

Sophie nodded, her investigative instincts sparking to life. "Thank you for telling me, Claire. I'll keep an eye out and... I'll be careful."

Claire's face softened, and she gave Sophie a small, grateful smile. "It's good to have someone who understands what's at stake. Just—don't let your guard down. This isn't as peaceful a place as it looks."

The tour was exactly what Sophie needed to reconnect with her passion. Claire explained winemaking's nuances, from soil to climate, and Sophie took notes, snapping photos and feeling a growing sense of inspiration for her blog and book.

They reached a small clearing at the back of the vineyard, where a bench sat beneath an ancient oak tree. The vineyard stretched out around them, a sea of green under the winter sky. Sophie took a deep breath, feeling more grounded than she had in ages.

"Mind if we sit for a bit?" Claire asked, gesturing to the bench.

"Not at all." Sophie settled beside her, soaking in the

peaceful scenery.

Claire seemed lost in thought before she spoke again. "You know, my uncle James... he's dedicated his life to this place. He practically raised me here after my parents passed. But recently, he's been... different. More stressed."

"Running a vineyard must be exhausting," Sophie offered gently. She could tell Claire had more on her mind.

"It is, but it's more than that. There's pressure to sell, and some family members think he should," Claire admitted, her voice tinged with frustration. "But, Uncle James says selling would betray everything our family's worked for. It's caused tension, especially with a few other vineyard owners eager to expand."

Sophie could see how deeply Claire cared about the vineyard and her uncle's vision. "Do you think he'll ever change his mind?"

"Honestly, I don't know," Claire replied, looking out over the vines. "He's stubborn, but he's also been more anxious lately. And then there's Angela. Let's just say Angela and my uncle have very different ideas about how things should be done."

"Sounds like they don't get along?"

"That's putting it lightly." Claire laughed. "Angela's all business. For her, it's about numbers and growth. She's been trying to buy out smaller vineyards for years, and I think my uncle is one of the few holdouts. It's like a game of cat and mouse at this point."

Sophie sensed that the "family drama" might be more than just business differences. There was something deeper here, though she didn't want to pry too much on only her second day.

After the tour, Claire invited her back to the main barn,

where workers were finishing up their tasks for the morning. Sophie took a few more photos of the equipment and workers, feeling a thrill as she thought about how she'd frame it all in her blog. Her readers would savor each detail of the vineyard's story.

Claire pulled out two glasses from a nearby table and poured them each a tasting of the vineyard's signature Pinot Noir. "It's a little early for wine, but we can make an exception."

Sophie raised her glass with a smile. "To new beginnings."

"To new beginnings," Claire echoed, clinking her glass against Sophie's.

The wine was rich, earthy, with a hint of cherry and spice. Sophie took a slow sip, letting the flavors linger. It tasted like the land itself—complex, rooted, timeless.

Just as they finished, the barn door opened, and a tall man with a weathered face and salt-and-pepper beard walked in. He carried himself with the ease of someone deeply connected to the land.

"Uncle James!" Claire called out, waving him over. "This is Sophie, our new neighbor. She's a food blogger and writer here to explore Sonoma's farm-to-table scene."

James offered Sophie a friendly but discerning smile. "Nice to meet you, Sophie. I hope Sonoma treats you well."

"Thank you," Sophie replied, feeling like she was being weighed and measured. "I've already fallen in love with the vineyard. It's breathtaking."

"Good to hear," he replied, his gaze shifting to the vines. "These vineyards carry generations of stories. Keeping it in the family means everything to us."

There was a quiet strength in his voice, a conviction that left no room for doubt. But Sophie noticed the faint lines of strain on his face, as though the weight of those generations pressed down daily.

The barn door swung open again, and a woman stepped in. She moved with purpose, her tailored blazer and polished demeanor stark against the rustic setting. Her gaze flicked to Sophie, then fixed on James with barely concealed irritation.

"James, we need to talk," Angela said, her voice clipped.

James's friendly demeanor faded, his jaw tightening. "Not now, Angela."

She crossed her arms, unperturbed. "This won't take long."

The tension between them was palpable. Sophie held her breath, wondering if she should excuse herself. Before she could, Angela's gaze shifted back to her.

"You must be the new neighbor," she said, a bitter smile playing on her lips. "Let me guess—a writer? A blogger, maybe?"

Sophie nodded politely. "Yes, I'm here for a few months to write about farm-to-table culture."

"Well, I hope you enjoy your stay," Angela replied, though her tone suggested otherwise. "Just remember, not all stories need to be told."

With that, she turned back to James. "We'll talk later, James. Don't keep avoiding it."

Angela strode out, leaving a tense silence in her wake. Sophie exchanged a glance with Claire, whose face reflected a mix of frustration and embarrassment.

"Sorry about that," Claire said. "Angela doesn't like hearing the word 'no.'"

Sophie tried to smile, though her mind was racing. She'd only been here a day, yet she was already sensing the layers of history, pride, and rivalry within this small community. Angela's words lingered, though she couldn't quite make sense of them.

As she walked back to the guesthouse that afternoon, Sophie's thoughts drifted to the tension she'd witnessed between James and Angela and the strain she'd glimpsed in James's eyes. It was just a hunch, but she couldn't shake the feeling that there was something deeper brewing beneath Sonoma's peaceful surface.

Back in the guesthouse, she pulled out her laptop and began jotting down notes, capturing the morning's tour, the vineyard's textures, and the tension she'd sensed in Claire and James. There was a story here—she could feel it.

For the first time in a long time, she felt the thrill of discovery stirring in her bones.

CHAPTER 3
SONOMA'S SECRETS

SOPHIE WOKE to a soft drizzle tapping against the windowpane, a gray mist blanketing the vineyard. As she pulled on a sweater and made her way to the kitchen, she felt a subtle thrill—a sense that beneath Sonoma's quiet charm, stories were waiting to be uncovered.

After brewing a steaming cup of coffee, she settled into the armchair by the window, watching the rain bead and roll down the glass. Angela's parting words lingered like a warning: Just remember, not all stories need to be told. It seemed Angela had strong feelings about her neighbor's legacy, and perhaps about Cartwright Vineyard itself.

Sophie sipped her coffee, mulling it over. Had she stumbled into a rivalry that ran deeper than business? She resolved to learn more about the relationships that connected—and divided—Sonoma's vineyard owners.

Later that morning, she grabbed her camera and notebook and made her way into town, hoping the market would offer a chance to run into some familiar faces. The drizzle had let up, leaving a thin veil of mist over the hills that gave the town an almost ethereal glow.

As she walked down the narrow path between the vines, the winter air held a faint chill, crisp and earthy, tinged with the wet-soil scent of the vineyard. Each step released a rich, loamy aroma that reminded her of freshly turned earth and hidden roots. She knelt briefly, pressing her hand into the damp soil, feeling its dense texture. Here, where everything grew in orderly rows yet carried a wildness beneath, she felt both grounded and unsettled.

The vines themselves stood in silent watch, their gnarled limbs stretching like ancient fingers toward the gray sky. A hush had settled over the vineyard, punctuated only by the rustle of dormant leaves and the creak of a nearby trellis. Sophie couldn't shake the feeling that something lingered in the shadows, a quiet presence like a whisper hovering just beyond hearing.

At the vineyard's edge, the stone fermentation cellar nestled into the hillside, looking dark and brooding. From here, she could smell the sharp, vinegary tang of fermenting wine drifting from the building's open door. As she approached, the hollow sounds of crates scraping against stone and murmurs from inside the cellar grew louder. For a moment, she hesitated, her instincts sensing that what lay ahead might be more than she had bargained for. But curiosity—or perhaps duty—urged her forward, into the vineyard's secrets.

Locals strolled through the market square, chatting and laughing as they browsed the stalls. Sophie gravitated to a stand overflowing with winter greens, herbs, and gleaming jars of preserves.

"Back for more already?" a voice called from behind.

She turned to see Claire approaching, her hair tucked under a knit hat and a basket of fresh produce in hand. "Guilty as charged," Sophie replied, grinning. "I thought I'd take in the market while it's still quiet."

Claire joined her at the stand, examining a bunch of rosemary. "Quiet mornings like this remind me of why I love this place, even with all the... drama."

"Drama?" Sophie raised an eyebrow. "I thought vineyards were supposed to be peaceful."

"Oh, they're peaceful—until people start fighting over them," Claire replied, a touch of bitterness in her voice. "My uncle's been under so much pressure lately. It's hard to watch."

Sophie's curiosity sharpened. "Do you mean pressure to sell? Angela mentioned expansion yesterday. She didn't seem too happy with your uncle's choices."

Claire sighed, her gaze shifting to the misty hills. "Angela's been trying to buy him out for years. She sees our vineyard as just another piece of her empire. But to Uncle James, it's so much more than that. It's his life, his legacy. He believes in doing things the right way. Angela... not so much."

Sophie felt an ache of understanding. She knew all too well the feeling of betrayal hidden under a veneer of trust. No more lies, she vowed silently, tightening her grip on her notebook. She couldn't erase her own past hurts, but she could do her part to prevent that kind of deception from tearing apart another family and legacy.

"I'll keep my eyes open," Sophie murmured, her voice low but resolute. "If Angela—or anyone else—tries anything, we'll be ready."

Claire's face softened with a grateful smile. "Just—don't get in too deep. This isn't as simple as it seems."

They wandered through the market together, Claire introducing her to vendors and friends. Sophie noted each person's story, all while keeping her ears open for any further hints about the Cartwrights' standing in the community.

At one point, they stopped at a small stall run by an older woman with silver hair swept into a loose bun, who sold hand-pressed olive oil. "You must be Sophie," the woman said, extending a hand. "I'm Maria."

"It's nice to meet you," Sophie replied, shaking her hand.

Maria's eyes twinkled as she looked between Sophie and Claire. "So, you're here to write about our little town, eh? Just be careful you don't go poking around where you're not wanted. Some stories are best left untold."

"Is that so?" Sophie asked with a smirk. "It wouldn't be the first time I've ignored a friendly warning."

Maria chuckled. "Then, you're braver than most who pass through here. We had a travel writer once who fancied himself a 'wine connoisseur.' He wouldn't stop blabbering about hints of 'forest floor' in his cabernet." Maria rolled her eyes. "Told him our cab had more hints of Sonoma dirt than anything else."

Claire snickered, and Sophie joined in. The camaraderie was infectious, and for a moment, the looming vineyard tension faded in the warmth of the town's peculiar humor.

"I'll keep that in mind," Sophie said with a grin. "I guess I should brush up on my wine-tasting vocabulary, or I'll be the next cautionary tale."

"Exactly, darling." Maria winked. "If you taste 'hints of leather,' it's probably just your shoes."

Sophie's heart skipped, but she masked her surprise. It seemed Maria shared Angela's sentiment about keeping certain matters private.

"Don't worry, Maria," Claire said, rolling her eyes. "Sophie's here for the food and culture, not to dig up dirt."

Maria chuckled. "We'll see about that. Writers always seem to find their way to the juiciest stories, whether or not they mean to."

Sophie laughed along, but the comment sat uneasily with her. Rather than deterring her, though, it only fueled her resolve to uncover the dynamics at play beneath Sonoma's charm.

After saying goodbye to Claire and Maria, Sophie wandered through the town square, snapping photos of the market stalls, ivy-covered buildings, and mist-shrouded hills. She paused by the stone fountain at the center of the square, contemplating the steady stream of water.

Her phone buzzed in her pocket. She pulled it out to see a message from Oliver.

> Oliver: All right, spill. How's the wine, and more importantly, how's the sleuthing? 🕵️

Sophie grinned and typed back.

> Sophie: Funny you should ask. I think I've found some Sonoma "drama." A local vineyard owner—Angela—is putting pressure on my landlord, Claire's uncle, to sell out. The whole town seems to be in on it. Everyone keeps warning me not to "poke around."

> Oliver: Ooh, a conspiracy in wine country! Just remember, they don't call it "liquid courage" for nothing. 🍷

She chuckled. There was something here worth protecting, and it went deeper than a simple rivalry.

> Sophie: I'll try to stay out of trouble. But, you know me—I'm basically a professional snoop.

> Oliver: It's what I love about you. Just don't get yourself kicked out before you've even unpacked.

She slipped her phone back into her pocket, Oliver's encouragement lingering in her mind like a warm spark. With her curiosity now fully engaged, Sophie decided to do a little "research." There was a library in town—a small stone building tucked into the square—and she had a hunch it might hold clues about the local vineyards' history.

The library was cozy, with wooden beams, reading nooks, and shelves lined with books that smelled faintly of dust and ink. Sophie searched the local history section, pulling out a few volumes before settling into a chair by the window.

It didn't take long to find references to the Cartwright

and Mason vineyards. Their rivalry, it turned out, went back decades. Cartwright Vineyard had been one of the first in the region, known for its traditional practices, while Mason Vineyard grew rapidly, becoming one of the largest distributors in the area. There were mentions of disputes over land, water rights, and even a legal battle over a parcel of land both families had once claimed.

As Sophie read, she pieced together a picture of the town's history—a delicate balance between preservation and progress, family legacies and business ambitions. And, at the heart of it all was Cartwright Vineyard, a symbol of the traditions Sonoma held dear.

The librarian approached, a kind-looking woman with round glasses and a warm smile. "Are you researching the vineyards?" she asked, peering at the titles on Sophie's table.

"Yes," Sophie replied. "I'm staying near Cartwright Vineyard and wanted to learn about its history."

The librarian nodded approvingly. "James Cartwright's family has been on that land for generations. People around here respect him a lot."

"And Angela Mason?" Sophie asked carefully.

The librarian's smile tightened. "Let's say she has a… different vision for the future."

Sophie tilted her head. "Do you think there's more to Angela's motives than just expansion?"

The librarian, Marjorie, lowered her voice. "Angela's father, Thomas, was determined to make Mason Vineyards a powerhouse, but he expanded too quickly and lost nearly everything in the '80s. Angela inherited her father's dreams—along with his debts. For her, this expansion isn't just business. It's a way to set her family's legacy right."

Marjorie sighed, glancing at the window. "It's not just James who feels the weight of this rivalry. The whole town does. People like Maria rely on James's vineyard not just for work but as a kind of heritage. Angela's expansion would threaten their livelihoods. That's why you'll find not everyone's on her side, even if she has the money."

Sophie thanked Marjorie and left the library with a notebook full of ideas—and more questions. It wasn't just a business rivalry. There was something about Cartwright Vineyard that stirred powerful feelings in everyone she'd met.

Back at the guesthouse, Sophie spread her notes across the dining table, circling key points and jotting down questions. As the rain pattered against the windows, she found herself absorbed in the mystery unfolding around her.

A knock at the door startled her from her thoughts. She crossed the room and opened the door to find a small envelope, sealed and unmarked, lying on the porch. She looked around, but no one was in sight. Puzzled, she picked it up and tore it open.

Inside was a single piece of paper with three words: Stay out, outsider.

A chill ran down her spine, but Sophie couldn't help a small smile. It seemed her questions had stirred more than she realized. This little town had its secrets, and she was just getting started.

CHAPTER 4
A PINCH OF SUSPICION

THE NOTE from last night sat on Sophie's table, its three words echoing in her mind: Stay out, outsider. After a final look, she slipped it into her bag, feeling her heart race—a mix of anger, fear, and stubborn resolve. Someone wanted to frighten her off, but if anything, the note only strengthened her determination.

Stepping out of the guesthouse, she dialed Claire's number. Her voice was steady but urgent. "Claire, meet me at the main barn. I have a few questions."

Moments later, she arrived at the barn to find Claire already waiting, her expression tense. Without hesitation, Sophie showed her the note. "This was on my doorstep last night."

Claire's face went pale. "Who… why would anyone do that?"

Sophie scanned the area, keeping her voice low. "Someone's trying to scare me off. But, they've only convinced me there's more going on here." She folded the note, slipping it back into her pocket. "I'm going to figure out who's behind this."

The morning had dawned bright and clear after yesterday's rain, and she decided to clear her mind with a walk through the vineyard. Rows of winter vines stretched toward the hills, framed by misty clouds lingering in the distance. The beauty of the place was undeniable, but now it seemed edged with something hidden.

She took out her phone and snapped a photo, then typed a caption draft for her blog: Sonoma has a quiet beauty, a sense of timelessness—but not everything here is as serene as it seems.

As she walked, she saw Claire up ahead, waving her over from the main path. "Sophie! Good timing. I was just about to check inventory in the barn. Want to join me?"

"Absolutely," Sophie replied, glad for the company.

Walking side by side, Sophie debated whether to mention the note but held off for now. Instead, she asked casually, "I noticed people seem... invested in the Cartwright-Mason rivalry. Maria had some strong opinions about 'poking around.'"

Claire rolled her eyes. "Ah, Maria. She's harmless but fiercely loyal to the 'old guard' around here, especially Uncle James. For people like her, Angela represents everything they don't."

Sophie nodded. "I can see why people might feel that way. It seems like the pressure on James is getting intense."

"It is," Claire admitted, a flicker of worry in her gaze. "He believes in preserving the vineyard's traditions, but he's struggling to keep up with modern demands. And with people like Angela breathing down his neck..." She trailed off, her frustration clear.

At the barn, Claire pulled open the heavy wooden doors, revealing rows of barrels, tools, and crates. The air smelled of aged wood and earth. She went to a clipboard hanging on the wall and checked the inventory list, her brow furrowed in concentration.

Sophie wandered around, taking in the neatly stacked barrels and gleaming tools. She snapped a few photos, already thinking about how she'd capture the scene for her readers. But, her attention drifted back to Claire, who studied the list with an intensity that suggested something unusual.

"Everything okay?" Sophie asked.

Claire sighed, setting down the clipboard. "Not really. A few recent shipments seem to be missing. It's just a few crates here and there, but... given everything else, it makes me uneasy."

Sophie's curiosity sharpened. "Do you think someone's taking them?"

Claire hesitated, then nodded. "It's possible. We've had the occasional bottle go missing during events, but this feels different. And with the recent tensions, I'm not ruling anything out."

"Does James know?"

"I mentioned it, but he's so preoccupied that he hasn't had time to look into it. He's hoping it's just a mistake, but I'm not so sure."

Sophie's mind raced. Theft, threats, missing inventory —it all seemed too coincidental. The note in her pocket felt like a warning about something larger. She kept her tone light. "Sounds like you could use a detective."

Claire gave her a small, grateful smile. "You're not wrong. Any help would be welcome."

Before Sophie could respond, footsteps sounded from outside, and James entered the barn, his expression serious as he looked between the two of them.

"Claire, Sophie," he greeted with a nod. "Didn't expect to find you both here."

"We're going over inventory," Claire said, masking her concern. "Some items are missing, but it's probably nothing."

James's gaze darkened, his jaw tightening. "We'll get it sorted. There's enough to worry about without adding inventory issues to the list." He turned to Sophie, his expression unreadable. "Sophie, I hope Sonoma's treating you well."

"Oh, it is," Sophie replied evenly. "Sonoma's beautiful. I can see why people are so passionate about this land."

James nodded, his gaze distant. "Passionate is one word for it. This land carries history—a legacy." He paused, choosing his words carefully. "But, legacies come with burdens."

There was a heaviness in his voice, a quiet strain that made Sophie wonder just how deep those burdens ran. She wanted to ask more, to press him about Angela and the pressures he faced, but she sensed that James wasn't ready to open up.

Instead, she simply nodded. "I understand. And, I think your dedication to this place is admirable."

His expression softened slightly, though the tension remained. "Thank you, Sophie. I appreciate that." He turned back to Claire. "I have a meeting with the bank later. Let's touch base about the inventory afterward. Keep this between us for now."

Claire nodded, though Sophie noted the worry in her face. Whatever was going on, James bore more weight than he was willing to share.

As James left the barn, Sophie and Claire exchanged a glance, an unspoken question between them. Before Sophie could say anything, Claire spoke up.

"Sophie, can I ask you something?" Her voice was quiet, uncertain.

"Of course," Sophie replied, sensing Claire's hesitation.

"Do you think… it's worth it to fight so hard to keep something everyone else wants you to let go of?" Claire's gaze was intense, searching.

Sophie considered her answer. "I think… if it's something that truly matters to you, it's worth fighting for. Even if others don't understand."

Claire gave her a small, sad smile. "That's what I thought, too. It's just hard when it feels like everyone's watching, waiting for us to fail."

Sophie placed a reassuring hand on Claire's arm. "You're stronger than you realize. And you're not alone in this."

For a moment, Claire seemed on the verge of saying more, but instead, she just nodded. They finished the inventory check in silence, each lost in thought.

As they left the barn, Sophie felt her own curiosity sharpen. She'd come to Sonoma to write about food, about farm-to-table traditions. But, it was clear that the story unfolding around her was more than she'd anticipated.

That night, back at the guesthouse, she pulled out her laptop and organized her notes. She wanted to piece together what she knew about the vineyard, Angela's ambitions, and the quiet resistance James represented.

Her phone buzzed. It was Oliver.

> Oliver: How's my little detective holding up? Still snooping around the grapevines? 🕵️‍♂️

Sophie smiled, his humor a comforting reminder she wasn't alone in her curiosity.

> Sophie: You know me—I can't let a mystery go unsolved.

> Oliver: Then keep digging. And don't forget to send me the juiciest bits for your book!

Sophie chuckled, his encouragement strengthening her resolve. The note had only fueled her determination.

As she looked out at the moonlit vineyard, a chill ran down her spine—but it only deepened her resolve. Whoever wanted her to stay out was about to find out that she had no intention of leaving this story unfinished.

CHAPTER 5
THE BITTER HARVEST

BY MID-MORNING, Sophie decided a walk through the vineyard might help clear her head. The sky had opened to a brilliant, cloudless blue, and the chilly air carried the earthy scent of damp soil. Despite the scene's beauty, her mind buzzed with questions about James, Angela, and the unseen pressures bearing down on Cartwright Vineyard.

The note's warning weighed on her thoughts. Someone didn't want her there, didn't want her asking questions. But rather than deterring her, it only fueled her curiosity. She wandered down a narrow dirt path, her eyes scanning the rows of dormant vines—like a quiet army standing guard over the family's secrets.

Her gaze fell on an irrigation pipe. The cut was clean, deliberate—a blatant act of sabotage. Her stomach twisted with unease. Someone was actively working to undermine James and, by extension, the Cartwright family legacy.

She snapped a quick photo for documentation, her mind racing. This was an escalation she couldn't ignore.

Finding Claire at the main house, Sophie's voice was a low murmur. "You need to see this. Someone's tampered with the irrigation pipes. This isn't just pressure to sell—this is a full-on campaign to wear James down."

Claire's eyes widened, her jaw setting in a line of resolve. "Then, we won't waste time. If they want a fight, we'll be ready."

As Sophie turned back toward the vineyard, an icy shiver ran down her spine. She caught a faint movement in the distance—a shadow slipping between the rows. Someone was close, and they weren't finished yet.

Rounding a bend, she spotted a figure bent over by one of the vines. Straightening, the person glanced her way, and she recognized Vincent, the vineyard worker she'd seen around the barn. He gave a curt nod but kept his focus on his work.

"Good morning," Sophie called, keeping her tone casual.

Vincent grunted, a sound that might have been a greeting. His rough hands and weathered face spoke of years of labor, and his gaze held a guarded look. She sensed he wasn't the type to chat with outsiders, but his perspective on the Cartwright family could be valuable.

"Beautiful day for working in the vineyard," she offered.

Vincent's gaze stayed on the vines. "Weather's fine, but vines don't care about that this time of year," he replied, his tone gruff.

"True." She nodded. "I suppose winter's more about maintenance?"

"Aye, that's about right," he replied, uninterested. But,

she noticed a faint flicker in his eyes—curiosity, perhaps, or irritation. Either way, it was something to work with.

"Claire mentioned a few crates have gone missing," Sophie ventured. "Has that happened before?"

His jaw tightened, and he glanced around, as if checking for eavesdroppers. "A crate here, a crate there," he muttered, keeping his voice low. "Nothing too unusual for a big operation. But—" His gaze shifted back to the vines, as if deciding how much to say.

"But?" Sophie prompted.

Vincent's eyes narrowed. "Things've been off lately. Used to be, we didn't worry about anyone taking as much as a bottle. But now… not everyone's as loyal as they pretend to be."

Sophie's pulse quickened. "Are you saying someone on the inside might be involved?"

Vincent shot her a sharp look and shook his head. "I'm saying nothing. Cartwright Vineyard looks after its own, and outsiders poking around won't change that."

With that, he turned back to his work, clearly dismissing her. Sophie took the hint, but his cryptic words left her mind buzzing with possibilities.

As she walked back toward the main path, her thoughts spun. Could someone within the vineyard be working against James? The missing crates, the family rivalry, and Vincent's guarded words all seemed to weave a web of intrigue around the Cartwrights.

She paid another visit to the town library. Perhaps digging into the Cartwright-Mason history might reveal more about the current pressures James faced.

The library was as quiet as ever, with soft sunlight filtering through tall windows. Sophie went straight to the local history section, pulling out the books she'd browsed before, this time hunting for details beyond the basics.

Flipping through an older volume, she found a brief article buried in the back pages of a decades-old local newspaper. It described a land dispute between the Cartwrights and the Masons, a court case settled in favor of the Cartwrights. The date was over thirty years old, but it suggested that the rivalry wasn't just about business—it was personal.

Just then, the librarian, Marjorie, approached with a knowing smile. "Back again, I see. Digging a little deeper, are we?"

Sophie smiled, nodding. "Just trying to get a sense of the town's history. The vineyard connections are fascinating."

Marjorie glanced at the page Sophie was reading. "The Cartwright-Mason feud goes back further than most realize. My grandmother used to tell me stories about those families. She'd say the Cartwrights were the town's heart, and the Masons... well, they were something else."

"Something else?" Sophie repeated, intrigued.

Marjorie leaned closer, lowering her voice. "Ambitious. Some would say ruthless. Angela Mason's just following a family legacy. The Masons always had big dreams—and they didn't let anything, or anyone, stand in their way."

Sophie thought of Angela's pointed remarks to James and the pressure she was putting on him to sell. It sounded as though Angela's ambitions weren't just about business; they were about winning a battle her family had been fighting for generations.

"Thanks for the insight, Marjorie," Sophie said, closing

the book. "It's interesting how much of a place's past is still present."

Marjorie nodded. "Don't hesitate to come back if you have more questions. Just... be mindful. Not everyone appreciates stirring up old ghosts."

Sophie left the library with fresh notes and the sense that the Cartwright-Mason rivalry was far more than a simple business dispute. The history seemed to hold clues to the pressures James faced—and possibly even the warning note on her doorstep.

Back at the guesthouse, she spread her notes across the table, sketching a diagram to map out connections she pieced together: the Cartwrights, the Masons, the land dispute, the missing inventory, and the constant pressure on James to sell.

Her phone buzzed, and she glanced at a new message from Oliver.

> Oliver: How's my favorite sleuth? Found any skeletons in the vineyard yet?

Sophie smiled, reassured by his humor.

> Sophie: Not yet, but the Cartwright-Mason rivalry runs deep. The Masons apparently have a reputation for getting what they want—at any cost.

> Oliver: Classic wine country drama. Just be careful, nosy writers don't usually get a warm reception.

> Sophie: Noted. But something's definitely off here. People keep warning me to "stay out," like they're all guarding some secret.

Oliver: Sounds like you're onto something. Just promise you'll keep your detective work subtle. We don't want you getting run out of town before you've hit the juiciest part.

Sophie took a deep breath and chuckled. Oliver's words lifted her spirits.

Later that afternoon, on her way back from town, she noticed Angela Mason's sleek black car parked outside the Cartwright property. Angela stood beside it, talking to James in low, heated tones. Sophie slowed, keeping to the edge of the vineyard, her attention on their tense exchange.

Angela gestured sharply, her voice carrying a tone of impatience. James shook his head, his stance rigid. The tension between them was almost tangible, an invisible wall between their opposing worlds.

Sophie took a cautious step closer, straining to hear when Angela's voice suddenly rose.

"James, you can't keep this up forever. Sooner or later, you'll have to let go of the past and think about what's best for everyone—especially Claire."

James's reply was too low for Sophie to catch, but the stubborn set of his shoulders was unmistakable. Angela huffed, clearly frustrated, before turning and climbing into her car. She drove off, kicking up a small cloud of dust in her wake.

As James turned to head back to the house, his gaze swept over the vineyard, his expression a mix of sadness and determination. Sophie could see the strain etched into his face—the burden of keeping the vineyard afloat against forces that seemed unrelenting.

Back at the guesthouse, Sophie jotted down a quick note of what she'd witnessed. The pieces were coming together, though she still couldn't see the full picture. But, she was closer than before, and one thing was certain: Angela Mason wasn't about to let the Cartwright legacy stand in her way.

Leaning back, Sophie studied her notes. Sonoma's peaceful facade was cracking, revealing something darker beneath. And despite the warnings, she knew she couldn't walk away now.

She was in too deep.

CHAPTER 6
STIRRING THE POT

THE NEXT MORNING, Sophie woke with a renewed sense of determination. In just a few days, Sonoma's idyllic veneer had cracked, revealing tensions bubbling beneath its picturesque vineyards. The Cartwright-Mason rivalry was deeper than she'd realized, and it seemed like everyone in town had a stake in keeping her in the dark.

After breakfast, she did a bit of investigating. Pulling on her coat, she headed to the main house to see if Claire or James was around. James's truck was gone, but Claire's car was in the driveway. Sophie knocked, and moments later, Claire opened the door, brightening when she saw her.

"Sophie! Come in," Claire said, stepping aside. "I was just making tea."

The kitchen felt inviting and cozy, filled with the scent of fresh herbs and a faint trace of wood smoke from the fireplace—a warm contrast to the tension simmering outside.

Claire poured her a cup, and they sat at the small

kitchen table. After a bit of small talk, Sophie eased into her questions.

"I ran into Vincent yesterday while he was working in the vineyard," Sophie began. "He mentioned that things have felt a bit... off lately."

Claire's smile faded, and she traced the rim of her teacup. "He's right. Things have been tense for a while now. Uncle James is under a lot of pressure—not just from the vineyard's demands."

Sophie leaned in. "Is it because of Angela?"

Claire nodded, a troubled look crossing her face. "Angela wants to expand, and she's determined to get her hands on this land. A few other vineyard owners sold to her years ago, so she has their backing. They see my uncle as the last holdout, the one person standing in the way of their 'progress.'"

"So, James is the only one who hasn't sold to her?"

"Exactly," Claire replied. "To him, selling would let down the family. This vineyard is a part of who he is. It's... complicated."

Sophie thought of the library records she'd found about the Cartwright-Mason land dispute, realizing this went beyond a business transaction. The weight of history seemed to press down on Claire and James, and Sophie felt a pang of empathy.

"I can see why he'd want to hold on," Sophie said. "But, it must be difficult with the pressure Angela's putting on him."

"It is," Claire admitted, her face clouding with worry. "And with the missing crates and other things going wrong lately, it feels like someone's trying to undermine him—to make him feel like he's losing control."

Sophie's mind whirred, processing this new angle. Angela—or someone on her behalf—might use under-handed tactics to rattle James and weaken his resolve.

"Have you told the authorities about the missing inventory?" Sophie asked carefully.

Claire shook her head. "Uncle James thinks it's just small-time theft and doesn't want to make a fuss. But... something about it feels deliberate."

Sophie made a mental note. The missing crates likely weren't random but a calculated push to destabilize James. And, the note she'd received, warning her to "stay out," had been another piece of that strategy.

Their conversation was interrupted when a car pulled up outside. Sophie looked out the window to see an unfamiliar black sedan, sleek and out of place against the rustic setting.

"Who's that?" Sophie asked, turning to Claire.

Claire's expression turned grim. "That's Peter Lawton. Angela's lawyer. He's probably here to push my uncle into selling."

Sophie's curiosity flared as they watched Peter step out of the car, his movements brisk and businesslike. He was tall and impeccably dressed, with an air of authority that suggested he was used to getting what he wanted. Claire seemed tense as Peter approached the main house.

"I'll give you some space," Sophie said, sensing Claire might prefer to handle this without an audience.

"No," Claire said, her voice firm. "Come with me. I'd feel better having someone else there."

Sophie nodded, sharing in her resolve. Together, they stepped outside to meet Peter, who waited on the porch with an expression of impatience and faint disdain.

"Peter," Claire greeted him coolly. "What brings you here?"

Peter gave a tight smile. "Angela asked me to speak with your uncle. Is he available?"

"He's not home right now," Claire replied, her tone polite but firm. "If you have a message, you can leave it with me."

Peter's gaze flicked to Sophie, an eyebrow raised in subtle disapproval. "And you are?"

"Sophie Brooks," she replied evenly. "A writer here to learn about Sonoma's farm-to-table culture."

Peter's expression remained impassive, but his eyes held a glint of suspicion. "A writer, you say? Interesting. Ms. Brooks, I'd advise you not to involve yourself in matters that don't concern you."

Sophie returned his gaze with a polite smile. "Thank you for the advice, Mr. Lawton, but I'm simply here as an observer. Cartwright Vineyard has a fascinating story, and I'm here to tell it."

Peter's lips tightened, but he turned back to Claire, his tone dismissive. "Let your uncle know that Angela's offer still stands, but time is running out. There are other interested parties, and we wouldn't want him to miss out on a generous deal."

Claire's eyes flashed with anger, but her tone remained controlled. "I'll let him know. Now, if you'll excuse us, we have work to do."

Without another word, Peter gave a curt nod, turned, and strode back to his car, his expression unreadable. They watched him drive off, the sound of gravel crunching under his tires, fading into the vineyard's quiet.

As the car disappeared, Sophie turned to Claire. "He's been by before, hasn't he?"

Claire nodded, frustration in her eyes. "Angela sends him every few weeks with a new 'generous' offer. She thinks if she pressures him enough, he'll cave. But, my uncle's as stubborn as they come."

"I admire his resolve," Sophie said sincerely. "It's not easy to stand up to someone with that much influence."

"Exactly," Claire replied, though worry softened her expression. "But, I don't know how much longer he can keep this up. Between the missing inventory, Angela's pressure, and managing the vineyard—it's only a matter of time before something gives."

Sophie nodded, sensing Claire's concern. The Cartwrights were under siege, and someone—or several someones—wanted to see James give in. The question was, how far would they go to make it happen?

As they headed back toward the barn, Sophie couldn't shake the feeling that she'd just witnessed a small piece of a much larger scheme. Angela's lawyer had made it clear that time was running out, and the undertone of his words suggested this was more than a financial transaction.

Back at the barn, Claire sighed, running a hand through her hair. "Sorry you had to see that. This whole situation has been… exhausting."

"Don't apologize," Sophie said with a reassuring smile. "I know how much this place means to you and your uncle. For what it's worth, I think you're doing an amazing job holding things together."

Claire managed a small, grateful smile. "Thanks, Sophie. It helps having someone around who understands."

They finished the inventory in companionable silence, Sophie glancing occasionally out at the vineyard as she processed everything she'd learned. Peter's warning and Angela's threats were taking shape as part of a larger, more menacing picture.

Later, back at her guesthouse, Sophie spread her notes across the table, reviewing the pieces she'd uncovered. The rivalry, the missing inventory, the lawyer's visit—each detail felt like a piece of a puzzle that pointed to something bigger than a business dispute.

As she organized her thoughts, her phone buzzed with a message from Oliver.

> Oliver: Hey there, Nancy Drew. What's the latest? 🍇

Sophie smiled, his humor a welcome reprieve.

> Sophie: Angela's lawyer just stopped by to deliver an "urgent" message. Looks like she's determined to buy the vineyard, whether or not James wants to sell.

> Oliver: Classic villain move. Sounds like you're getting close to the heart of this. Remember, the good guys always win. 😉

> Sophie: Let's hope so. I have a feeling this is just the beginning.

> Oliver: Stay safe, and keep me posted. Sonoma's secrets don't stand a chance.

Sophie set her phone down. She was in the middle of something bigger than she'd expected, but she wasn't backing down. Sonoma's secrets were surfacing—and she was ready to uncover them all.

CHAPTER 7
LAYERS OF GUILT

THE SUN WAS SETTING, casting long shadows across Cartwright Vineyard, as Sophie walked back to the guesthouse. Her conversation with Claire and the unsettling visit from Angela's lawyer, Peter, replayed in her mind. It was obvious that Angela's camp was ramping up the pressure on James, willing to go to any lengths to secure the land. Each interaction left Sophie more convinced there was a bigger game at play—and she was more determined than ever to uncover it.

Later that evening, she sat at her small table, skimming through her notes and mapping out the key players in this twisted situation. Angela wasn't just pressuring James herself; she had allies in town, each subtly pushing him toward a decision. Sophie was beginning to suspect that some locals were quietly supporting Angela's plans, perhaps even nudging James in her direction.

A knock on the door interrupted her thoughts. Surprised, Sophie opened it to find Nate standing there, a warm smile on his face and a small bag of groceries in hand.

"Nate! What brings you by?" she asked, touched by his unexpected visit.

"Thought you might need a few essentials," he said, holding up the bag. Inside was fresh-baked bread, local olive oil, and a small bottle of wine. "Consider it a Sonoma welcome kit for our resident writer."

Sophie grinned. "That's so thoughtful, thank you."

Nate stepped inside, setting the bag on her counter as he looked around at the rustic charm of the guesthouse. "So, how's Sonoma treating you? Has it cast its spell yet?"

"Oh, absolutely," Sophie said, pouring them each a glass of wine. "It's beautiful, peaceful... and more than a little mysterious."

Nate chuckled, taking a seat at the table. "Mysterious, huh? You mean the Cartwright-Mason feud?"

Sophie nodded, joining him. "Everyone seems to have strong opinions about it. Even strangers are telling me to stay out, which only makes me more curious."

"Can't blame you," Nate replied, leaning back. "Around here, family loyalty and history are everything. And with the Cartwrights and Masons... well, most folks would rather leave the past buried."

"Why's that?" Sophie pressed, sensing that Nate might have a unique perspective.

Nate hesitated, swirling his wine. "It's about more than vineyards. James represents a way of life that's disappearing. Angela wants to turn Sonoma into something bigger, something commercial. Some people support her vision—new jobs, more business—but they don't want to be the ones to say it."

Sophie frowned, the pieces starting to click into place. "So, they let Angela be the face of it?"

"Exactly. Angela's ambitions might seem ruthless, but she's just saying out loud what others are too polite—or too cautious—to say. Sonoma's charm is in its simplicity, but change is coming, and some believe her way is the only way forward."

"So, James is an obstacle to progress?" Sophie asked, realizing just how divided this conflict was.

Nate shrugged. "Depends on who you ask. Some see him as a hero, others as a stubborn old man clinging to the past. But, he's under a lot of pressure, and if he won't sell willingly..." Nate let the implication hang.

Sophie took a thoughtful sip of her wine. "You think Angela and her allies might try to force his hand?"

"Wouldn't surprise me," Nate said, his voice darkening. "Angela's got backing in town, business owners who'd benefit if she took over. I've even heard rumors that some of James's employees might work with her, making it harder for him to keep up."

Sophie's mind buzzed with this new information. Angela had built herself a coalition, positioning her ambitions as progress. If she couldn't win James over directly, she'd chip away at his support until he had no choice.

"Any idea who her allies are?" Sophie asked, keeping her tone casual.

Nate hesitated, studying her for a moment. "I'm not sure I should share town gossip with a mystery writer." He gave her a teasing grin, though Sophie caught the caution in his tone.

"Oh, come on," she replied, nudging him with her glass. "I'm harmless. Just a writer looking for inspiration."

"Uh-huh," Nate said, his grin widening. "Well, if you're that curious… I'd keep an eye on Vincent."

"Vincent?" Sophie's eyebrows shot up. "The vineyard worker?"

"Yep. He's been with the Cartwrights for years, and I thought he was loyal to James. But lately, he's been spending a lot of time with Angela's crew. Wouldn't surprise me if she made him an offer he couldn't refuse."

Sophie considered this. Vincent's guarded words the other day had hinted at loyalty, but there'd been an edge to his tone—a bitterness she hadn't placed. If he was working with Angela, the missing crates and recent issues could be sabotage from within.

"Nate, I owe you one," she said, grateful for the insight.

"Don't mention it," he replied, raising his glass. "Just don't get yourself into trouble. I like having a mystery writer as a neighbor."

They clinked glasses, and Sophie couldn't help but smile at his warmth. After he left, she sat back, piecing together what she'd learned. Vincent—was he betraying James? And if so, what had Angela offered him in return?

The next day, she found Vincent tending to the vines, his back turned as he pruned some of the older branches. Taking a steadying breath, she approached him.

"Morning, Vincent," she called, aiming to keep things light.

He turned, giving her a guarded nod. "Morning."

"Mind if I join you for a bit?" she asked, stepping closer. "I could use a refresher on vine care."

Vincent shrugged, motioning for her to join him. "Suit yourself."

They worked in silence, Sophie mimicking his movements as he pruned. She felt him watching her out of the corner of his eye, likely wondering what brought her there.

After a few minutes, she took a chance. "I hear things have been... tense, lately."

Vincent's jaw tightened, his pruning motions growing sharper. "What's it to you?"

"Just curious," Sophie replied, keeping her tone even. "Seems like everyone has strong opinions about what should happen with the vineyard. And, Angela doesn't strike me as someone who takes 'no' lightly."

Vincent snorted, clearly unimpressed. "Angela doesn't care about this place. She only cares about what she can make off it."

Sophie hesitated, then pushed further. "I heard she's made offers to people around town. Promises of jobs, better wages. Has she approached you?"

Vincent's eyes flashed, and for a moment she thought he might snap. But, he just shrugged, his expression hardening. "People here do what they have to do to survive. Some think Angela's got the right idea. I've got a family to feed."

The weight of his admission hung between them. Whatever Vincent's original loyalties, Angela seemed to have found a way to sway him, using Sonoma's economic struggles to her advantage.

"Do you think it's worth it?" Sophie asked quietly. "Trading away something that's been here for generations?"

Vincent's gaze hardened. "What would you know about it? You're just here to take pictures and write stories.

Some of us..." He stopped, pressing his lips together as if he'd said too much.

"I may be an outsider, Vincent," Sophie said, steadying her voice, "but I know what it's like to want to protect something, even if others don't understand."

For a second, a flicker of doubt crossed his face. But then, he shook his head, the guarded look returning. "You don't know anything about it. You'd do well to leave it alone, Ms. Brooks."

He turned his back, resuming his work with renewed focus, a clear sign the conversation was over.

Sophie walked away, her mind racing. Vincent was torn—loyalty, survival, pride, and pressure all tangled up in his heart. And, Angela exploited that, positioning herself as a "savior", while quietly dividing James's supporters.

As she made her way back to the guesthouse, her phone buzzed with a message from Oliver.

> Oliver: How's Sonoma's most meddlesome resident? Stirring up trouble yet? 🦝

Sophie grinned at his humor, a welcome relief after her tense exchange.

> Sophie: A bit. I think I've found Angela's weak spot—she's using people like Vincent to pressure James.

> Oliver: Classic villain move. Maybe you should wear a cape next time you snoop.

Sophie laughed, picturing herself sweeping through the vineyards in a dramatic cape.

> Sophie: Tempting. I'll keep the cape idea in mind.

> Oliver: And a monocle! Sonoma wouldn't know what hit it. Or borrow my trench coat—I'll even throw in my "Serious Detective" hat.

> Sophie: I'll consider it. But for now, blending in works fine. Keep the hat ready, though.

> Oliver: Done. Watson on standby. 🍷

Tucking her phone away, Sophie felt her resolve deepen even more. This wasn't just a feud over land; it was a battle for the soul of Sonoma, and she was determined to uncover every secret it held.

CHAPTER 8
SPICED WITH SECRETS

A BITING wind rattled the vines outside Sophie's guesthouse as she sat at her table, poring over her notes. Her conversation with Vincent had deepened the mystery; he wasn't the only one under Angela's sway, but he was the first to openly hint at what Angela was offering—a lifeline, a promise of stability in a town where tradition often clashed with change.

Sophie leaned back, staring at the list of names she'd assembled: Vincent, Angela, Peter the lawyer… Each had a stake in forcing James out. And, the anonymous note—Stay out, outsider—still lingered in her mind. Was it a warning or a threat? The more she considered it, the more it felt like a piece of a larger, orchestrated scheme.

Her phone buzzed on the table, breaking her concentration. She smiled at the message from Oliver.

> Oliver: Detective Sophie Brooks, I presume? Any new leads in the Great Grape Heist?

> Sophie: The plot thickens. Angela's been pressuring half the town to back her plans, and I think someone's actively sabotaging James—missing inventory, "accidental" damage, even notes warning me to back off.

> Oliver: Sounds like you're right back in the deep end, just like old times. But remember, you've come a long way. Sonoma's lucky to have you in its corner.

Oliver's words warmed her. Somehow, he always knew when to remind her of how far she'd come.

> Sophie: Thanks, Oliver. Honestly, it feels different this time. I know I'm on my own, but I feel...stronger. Like this is exactly where I need to be.

> Oliver: That's the Sophie I know. You've been through worse and come out stronger. Just don't let people like Angela make you doubt yourself. This is your story now.

His encouragement settled her resolve. This was her story, her choice.

After ending the exchange, Sophie headed to the Cartwright house. She wanted to talk to James directly. If anyone could shed light on Angela's methods and the town's shifting loyalties, it was him. She sensed he knew more than he'd been willing to share.

As she approached the main house, she saw Claire on the porch, looking lost in thought. Claire's face brightened when she noticed her.

"Sophie! Just the person I wanted to see," Claire said, beckoning her over.

"What's going on?" Sophie asked, picking up on a hint of unease.

"It's... Uncle James. He's been so tense lately. More than usual. I'm worried all this pressure is really taking a toll."

Sophie nodded, understanding. "I actually wanted to ask him a few questions. Do you think he'd be open to talking?"

Claire hesitated, then nodded. "Yes, I think he would. But... just go easy on him. He doesn't like showing weakness."

"Of course," Sophie assured her. "I'll keep it gentle."

Claire led her inside to James's study. She knocked softly, and after a muffled "Come in," opened the door for Sophie to step inside.

James sat at a large wooden desk, papers spread out in front of him. He looked up, his expression hardening slightly when he saw her.

"Sophie," he greeted her cautiously. "To what do I owe the pleasure?"

"I wanted to ask a few questions," Sophie said carefully. "I know Angela's been putting pressure on you, and it seems her influence runs deep in this town. But, what I don't understand is... why so many people are quick to take her side."

James leaned back in his chair, rubbing a hand over his face. "Sonoma isn't what it used to be," he said, his voice weary. "It used to be about community, working together, preserving what we had. Now it's about who can make the most money, the fastest."

He gestured to the papers on his desk—documents, invoices, what looked like bills and mortgage statements. "Angela knows exactly where to strike. She's offering people what they need—jobs, stability, a way out of debt— turning them against me one by one."

Sophie's eyes lingered on the documents, the mounting financial strain clear. "That's why she's targeting the vineyard?"

"Exactly," James said, bitterness creeping into his tone. "She wants me to feel like I'm fighting a losing battle, like I don't have the resources to hold on. She's got allies in town—people who benefit if I sell and who'd love nothing more than to see me fall."

Sophie felt a pang of empathy as she took in the lines etched into his face, the weight of his family's legacy pressing heavily on his shoulders.

"James," she said gently, "have you thought about going to the authorities? Reporting the missing inventory, the pressure?"

He shook his head, his expression resolute. "What good would it do? I can't prove anything, and Angela has friends in high places. They'd brush it off as coincidence, or bad luck."

Sophie wanted to press him, but his set jaw made it clear he wasn't willing to take that step. She glanced at a dusty photo frame on his desk—a picture of James and a young Claire, their faces bright with laughter as they stood among the vines. This vineyard was more than a business; it was their home, their history.

"Thank you, James," she said sincerely. "I just want you to know... you're not alone in this. Claire cares deeply about this place. And so do I."

James's expression softened slightly, and he gave her a small nod. "I appreciate that, Sophie. More than you know."

As she left the house, Sophie felt a renewed sense of purpose. Angela might have power, but with each conversation, each new clue, Sophie could see cracks in her plan.

But, her confidence was soon tested. Returning to the guesthouse, Sophie noticed the door slightly ajar. Her heart skipped as she stepped closer, peering inside.

The room was in disarray—papers, notes, even her laptop scattered across the floor. Someone had rifled through her things.

Her pulse quickened as she stepped carefully inside, scanning the room for anything missing. Her mind raced —could it have been Peter, or another of Angela's allies, trying to scare her off?

She knelt to gather her notes and noticed a slip of paper on the floor. It was a hastily written note left in plain sight: Leave while you still can.

The words were scrawled in bold, angry letters, unmistakable in their threat. Sophie's hands trembled slightly as she held the note. This wasn't just a warning—it was a threat from someone who wanted her gone.

Her phone buzzed, and she pulled it out to see a message from Oliver.

Oliver: Just checking in. Still alive, right?

Sophie took a steadying breath, typing back quickly.

> Sophie: Barely. Someone broke into my guesthouse and left me a note: "Leave while you still can."

Oliver's reply was instant.

> Oliver: WHAT? Sophie, this isn't a game. Are you sure you're safe there?

> Sophie: Yes. It's unsettling, but I won't let them scare me off. I'm too close to figuring this out.

> Oliver: Promise me you'll be careful. This is starting to sound dangerous.

> Sophie: I promise. And I'll keep you updated.

After the exchange, Sophie surveyed the mess, her mind racing. Walking away might be the safe choice, but she couldn't do it. The Cartwrights needed her, and this mystery was hers to uncover.

Whoever had broken in feared what she might find. And that fear was all the encouragement she needed to keep pushing forward.

She spent the rest of the evening organizing her notes, her determination hardening with each piece of evidence she laid out. Angela and her allies might be powerful, but Sophie wasn't backing down.

As night fell, she looked out at the dark silhouettes of the grapevines, feeling their presence like silent sentinels. The note's threat echoed in her mind: Leave while you still can. It wasn't just a warning—it was a promise. Someone out there was watching, waiting, and prepared to do anything to keep her quiet. But she'd come this far, and no threat could make her turn back now.

CHAPTER 9
THE GRAPES OF RIVALRY

EVER SINCE THE BREAK-IN, Sophie couldn't shake the feeling of being watched. Every creak of the guesthouse, every shadow outside her window, every hushed conversation in the town square seemed amplified, almost as if Sonoma itself was pushing her out. Leave while you still can. The note's words echoed in her mind, but instead of deterring her, they fueled her determination. Someone was hiding secrets, and she was getting close to uncovering them.

By mid-morning, Sophie decided her next move was a visit to Maria, the vendor from the farmers' market who had her finger on the pulse of the town's secrets. If anyone knew more about Angela's alliances, it would be her.

The market bustled as usual, with locals browsing winter produce and sampling cheeses and honey. The familiar scent of roasted chestnuts filled the air, mingling with the crisp bite of the season. Sophie spotted Maria at her olive oil stall, pouring samples for a customer.

"Maria!" Sophie greeted, approaching with a warm smile.

Maria's face lit up. "Ah, Sophie! Back for more of my olive oil?"

"Always," Sophie replied, accepting a small sample cup. She took a sip, savoring the rich, peppery taste. "It's the best I've ever had."

Maria laughed, a twinkle in her eye. "I've been told it's the secret to long life and good gossip."

Sophie chuckled, then leaned in. "Speaking of gossip… I was hoping you could help me. I'm trying to understand more about the Cartwright-Mason feud. It feels like there's more to it than just business."

Maria's smile faded, her gaze shifting around cautiously. She lowered her voice. "You're right, dear. It's personal—and it goes back generations. Angela's family always wanted more land, more power. But the Cartwrights are stubborn. James would rather die than sell."

"What about Angela? She seems to have a lot of support," Sophie pressed.

Maria sighed, nodding. "Angela's good at making promises. Jobs, better wages—things people can't easily turn down. But, don't let her fool you; she's only interested in power and control."

Sophie absorbed this, her mind racing. Angela's reach was more deeply rooted than she'd realized. But, who among James's employees had switched sides?

"Have you heard if anyone from the vineyard might have… joined her?" Sophie asked carefully.

Maria hesitated, her gaze wary. "You didn't hear this

from me, but people say Vincent's been seen around Angela's property. Visiting her office, even meeting with her lawyer, Peter. He's been with the Cartwrights for years, but... money can change anyone."

Sophie's pulse quickened. If Vincent was secretly working with Angela, it could explain the missing inventory and other "accidents" at the vineyard.

"Thank you, Maria," Sophie said sincerely. "I'll keep that to myself."

Maria's expression turned somber. "Be careful, Sophie. There are things in this town best left alone. I'd hate to see you get hurt."

Sophie managed a reassuring smile. "I'll be careful. Promise."

With Maria's words lingering in her mind, Sophie left the market and headed back to the vineyard, determined to confront Vincent.

Later that afternoon, she found him near the maintenance shed, stacking crates with his usual, gruff efficiency. She took a deep breath and approached, trying to keep it casual.

"Hey, Vincent!" she called, giving him a friendly wave.

He turned, his face as guarded as ever. "What do you need?"

Sophie forced a smile. "Just wanted to thank you for showing me the ropes the other day. I had no idea how much work goes into a place like this."

Vincent's expression softened slightly. "It's honest work," he muttered, a trace of pride in his voice.

"I respect that," Sophie replied. "It must mean a lot to you, working here all these years."

Vincent's jaw tightened, his gaze flicking away. She caught a glimmer of something in his eyes—guilt, maybe? Resentment?

"It's a job, same as any other," he replied tersely.

Sophie hesitated, then took a chance. "I heard a rumor you've been meeting with Angela Mason. It just seems... odd, given the history with the Cartwrights."

His face flushed, and he turned away, busying himself with the crates. "People love to talk. They don't know what they're saying half the time."

"Maybe," Sophie replied, keeping her tone neutral. "But, I can see why someone might feel caught between two sides. Angela's offering security—that's hard to turn down."

He froze, his hands stilling on a crate. When he looked at her, his expression was pained. "I have a family, Sophie. I can't just put loyalty above everything."

Sophie's suspicion softened into empathy. "I get it, Vincent. And, I don't blame you. Times are tough, and Angela's powerful. But... I hope you know what you're getting into."

For a moment, he looked like he might say something more. But then, he turned abruptly, heading back to his work, leaving Sophie with more questions than answers.

That evening, Sophie felt she'd hit a wall with Vincent. He wasn't ready—or able—to tell her more. She stopped by Nate's restaurant, hoping he might offer insights into the local dynamics. Nate had a way of seeing through the town's facades, and she suspected he knew more than most.

The cozy restaurant buzzed with warmth and the inviting aroma of roasted garlic and herbs. Nate was slicing bread behind the bar when he spotted her and waved her over, a grin spreading across his face.

"Sophie! Perfect timing," he said, gesturing to a seat at the bar. "Let me get you something. On the house."

She returned his smile. "Thanks, Nate. I could use it."

He placed a steaming bowl of mushroom risotto and a glass of red wine in front of her. Sophie took a sip, the rich flavors settling her nerves.

"So," Nate said, leaning across the bar. "Something tells me you didn't come here just for the food."

Sophie laughed, grateful for his insight. "You caught me. I actually wanted to ask more about the vineyard and Angela's… influence."

Nate raised an eyebrow, his expression turning serious. "Word's going around someone broke into your guest-house. Is that true?"

Sophie blinked, surprised at how quickly news spread in town. "Yeah. They left me a note, too. Something like 'leave while you still can.'"

Nate's face darkened, his jaw clenching. "I knew Angela had her claws in people, but intimidation? That's low, even for her."

"Angela's not exactly subtle," Sophie replied. "But, I think there's more at play. Do you know who's helping her?"

Nate glanced around, as if making sure no one was listening, then leaned in. "Angela's got a network. Mostly people tired of the old ways, who think she's their ticket to a modern town—even if it means selling out Sonoma's charm."

"Do you know their names?" Sophie asked, lowering her voice.

Nate hesitated, casting a cautious glance at the door. "Vincent's in her camp. And Greg Sanders, from the hardware store. He's been pushing for change for years. Then there's Peter Lawton, her lawyer—he handles her dirty work, from property disputes to… other issues."

Sophie's mind raced. Angela's coalition was larger than she'd expected, and it painted a bleak picture of Sonoma's future if she succeeded. This wasn't just about a vineyard —it was about reshaping the town, with Angela at the helm.

Nate's voice softened. "Look, Sophie, I know you're trying to help, but Angela doesn't like interference."

Sophie managed a smile. "I'm starting to see that. But, I'm not stopping until I get to the truth."

Nate sighed, a hint of admiration in his expression. "I figured you'd say that. Just… be careful. Angela has a way of making problems disappear."

She finished her meal, thanked him, and headed back to the guesthouse, feeling both enlightened and uneasy. Angela was more dangerous than she'd realized, and her coalition of supporters was more than willing to keep her in power.

Back at the guesthouse, Sophie spread out her notes, highlighting the names Nate had given her—Vincent, Greg Sanders, Peter Lawton. Angela had maneuvered these people into her orbit, promising them a brighter future if they aligned with her. But, Sophie sensed a crack in her coalition, a sliver of doubt that she could exploit.

A faint rustling near the back door broke her focus. Sophie froze, her heart pounding as she listened to the slow, cautious footsteps approaching outside. She glanced at her phone, her hand hovering over it, ready to call for help.

Then, silence.

After a tense pause, she heard footsteps recede, followed by a crunch of gravel. She exhaled shakily, moving toward the door to check. The porch was empty, but lying on the ground was a small envelope with a single word scrawled across it: Enough.

Inside was a single piece of paper, the message in messy, bold handwriting: Stay out of Angela's business, or the next warning won't be so gentle.

A chill ran down her spine. This wasn't just a warning —it was a final notice.

Her phone buzzed, and she saw a message from Oliver.

Oliver: Just checking in. Still alive, right?

Sophie took a steadying breath, typing back quickly.

Sophie: Barely. Someone left me another note: "Leave while you still can."

Oliver: This isn't a game, Sophie. Be careful.

Sophie: I'm on it. I think I'm close to something big.

She put her phone down, her resolve hardening. Angela's coalition might be powerful, but they didn't understand that their threats only strengthened her determination. Tomorrow, she'd confront James again. She needed every piece of information if she was going to take on Angela and her allies.

As she lay in bed that night, thoughts of Sonoma, the Cartwrights, and Angela's web of influence kept her awake. She had no intention of leaving until every secret was brought to light.

This was a battle she was willing to fight to the very end.

CHAPTER 10
SALT IN THE WOUND

THE MORNING DAWNED gray and quiet, a thick fog hanging low over Cartwright Vineyard. Sophie sipped her coffee, her mind running through the plan she'd formed. The threatening note had rattled her, but it had also solidified her determination. Angela's network of supporters wanted her silenced, and if they were that desperate, then she was close to exposing something crucial.

She finished her coffee, pulled on her coat, and set off for the main house. It was time for answers, and she intended to get them today—whether or not James was ready.

Sophie found James hunched over a pile of documents in the study, his face lined with stress. He looked up as she entered, managing a tired smile.

"Sophie. What brings you here this early?"

She closed the door behind her, taking a deep breath. "I need answers, James. Angela's supporters are threatening me, and I know she's got people like Vincent and Peter Lawton in her corner, along with some of the town's business owners. I can't help you if I don't know the whole story."

James's jaw tightened as he looked away, a flicker of pain crossing his face. "I never wanted you caught up in this. This vineyard... it's all I have left of my family's legacy. Angela knows that."

"Then, why let her continue this campaign?" Sophie asked gently. "There has to be something—some proof of what she's doing."

James looked defeated. "Angela's careful. She's been planning this for years, pulling strings, and covering her tracks. Her supporters will do whatever it takes to see me forced out."

"Let me help find that proof," Sophie urged. "She has to have slipped up somewhere."

James was silent, his gaze distant, as though weighing his options. Finally, he nodded. "There's one thing. My father kept a journal—he wrote every major decision, every interaction with the Masons, every dispute over the land. If anyone knew the lengths Angela's family would go to, it was him."

"Where's the journal?" Sophie asked, her heart quickening.

James gestured to a large, locked cabinet in the corner. "It's there. I haven't looked at it in years."

He retrieved a small key, unlocked the cabinet, and pulled out a worn, leather journal, its cover cracked with age. He handed it to Sophie, his gaze solemn. "If you're set on digging up the past, here it is."

Sophie flipped through the journal's pages, each one filled with careful notes in James's father's handwriting. She scanned the entries, and one line caught her eye—a mention of a large "settlement" from Angela's father, paid to drop a legal dispute.

"James," Sophie said, her voice tinged with excitement. "This 'settlement'… it sounds like a bribe. Your father might have been pressured to drop his case against Angela's family years ago. Maybe she's using the same tactic now."

James's frown deepened as he examined the entry. "I never knew about this payment. My father never mentioned it. But, it wouldn't surprise me if Angela's picking up where her father left off."

Sophie nodded. "If we can find records of similar payments to Vincent or other business owners, that could be the proof we need."

James's face hardened with resolve. "There's a storage room in the barn with the vineyard's old records. I haven't thought to look there, but it's worth a try."

They spent hours sifting through old ledgers and invoices in the dusty storage room, the silence punctuated only by the occasional rustle of paper. Finally, Sophie found a line item that looked out of place—a large payment made to Greg Sanders, the hardware store owner, just a few months prior.

She showed it to James, who scowled. "Greg's one of Angela's strongest supporters. But, I didn't think he'd take money from her."

Sophie's pulse quickened. This was the proof they needed—evidence linking Angela to one of her allies in the town. They combed through more recent records, and soon enough, uncovered similar payments to other local businesses, each labeled as "consulting fees" or "invest-ments" in vague "development" projects.

Sophie's heart raced. Angela had been buying influence, paying off the town's business owners to pressure James into selling.

"This is it, James," she said, her voice brimming with excitement. "Angela's been bribing people, trying to wear you down and cut off your support."

James's expression shifted, a mixture of relief and determination. "It's time the town knew the truth."

By afternoon, word had spread that James was making an announcement in the town square. A small crowd gathered, faces marked with curiosity and anticipation. Sophie stood beside James, clutching the evidence they'd uncovered, feeling both exhilarated and anxious.

James stepped forward, holding the journal and a stack of documents. He cleared his throat, his voice steady as he addressed the townspeople.

"I know many of you have heard Angela's promises of prosperity and change," he began, his gaze sweeping over the crowd. "But, what you may not know is the cost of her ambition."

He held up the documents Sophie had uncovered. "These are payments Angela has made to several businesses in town—payments disguised as 'consulting fees' and 'investments.' She's been buying support, isolating me so I'd feel forced to sell."

A murmur rippled through the crowd, faces shifting from curiosity to shock. Sophie caught sight of Greg Sanders, pale and visibly uncomfortable, shifting from foot to foot. A few other business owners exchanged uneasy glances.

Claire stepped forward, her voice calm but resolute.

"This vineyard is more than land. It's our family's history. We won't let Angela destroy it for her own interests."

Just then, a sleek, black car pulled up at the edge of the square. Angela Mason stepped out, her expression cool but her eyes hard as she approached James.

"What exactly are you accusing me of, James?" she asked, her voice laced with disdain.

James held her gaze, unwavering. "I'm accusing you of bribery, Angela. Of paying off the town to isolate me, to pressure me into selling. I have the documents to prove it."

Angela's lips tightened, but she managed a practiced smile. "I think you're reading into things, James. All I've done is invest in local businesses. Isn't that what any responsible business owner would do?"

Sophie spoke up, her voice steady. "Investment is one thing, Angela. But, buying loyalty and forcing people to take sides? That's manipulation."

Angela's mask slipped, a flicker of anger flashing in her eyes. But, she quickly regained her composure, her voice low. "This isn't over, James. You may have put on a show, but I always get what I want."

With that, she turned and walked back to her car, leaving the crowd in stunned silence.

Sophie knew they'd won a battle, but Angela's parting words lingered ominously in her mind. This wasn't over. Not by a long shot. But, for the first time since arriving in Sonoma, Sophie felt hopeful. They had exposed Angela, and now the town knew the truth.

She stood beside James and Claire in the fading light. They'd faced Angela's power and prevailed, but she knew this was only the beginning.

Angela Mason wasn't finished yet—and neither was Sophie.

CHAPTER 11
THE SOUR TRUTH

THE TOWN SQUARE felt different the next morning. Word had spread about the confrontation between James and Angela, and Sophie sensed the shift as she walked through the market. Some locals offered nods of encouragement, others whispered behind her back, while a few avoided her entirely. Sonoma was split, its loyalties divided between those who respected James's resolve and those captivated by Angela's promises.

At Cartwright Vineyard, the mood was tense. Sophie joined James and Claire in the kitchen, where shadows stretched across the worn wooden table. They were still reeling from the previous day's events, but it was clear they were bracing for Angela's next move.

"She won't take this lying down," James muttered, his tone both frustrated and resolute. "Angela's dug her claws in too deep. She won't just walk away."

Claire nodded, frowning. "Do you think she'll retaliate? Maybe try to discredit us?"

Sophie shared a look with James and nodded. "Most

likely. Her power comes from her connections, and she'll use whatever influence she has to turn people against you."

Just then, a knock sounded at the door. Claire opened it to find Nate standing there, slightly out of breath, worry etched across his face.

"Nate?" she asked, concern tightening her tone. "Is everything all right?"

"Not exactly." Nate stepped inside, his face drawn. "Angela's calling a meeting tonight at the town hall. Word is, she plans to 'address' the situation with the Cartwrights."

Sophie's stomach clenched. The play was as she had expected. Angela would rally her supporters, casting doubt on the Cartwrights' claims and pulling undecided townsfolk to her side.

"We have to be there," Sophie said, her voice hardening. "If she's rallying her supporters, she's not going to hold back."

A heavy silence settled among them, the gravity of the impending confrontation weighing on each of them. Sophie could almost feel Angela's influence weaving through the town, binding people with both loyalty and fear. Whatever Angela planned, one thing was clear—she wasn't preparing to lose.

James nodded grimly. "If she's calling this meeting, it means she's afraid of losing control. But, I'd be lying if I said I wasn't worried about what she might try."

By the time they arrived at the town hall, the place was packed. Locals filled the seats, their expressions a blend of curiosity, tension, and, sometimes, open hostility. Sophie felt the charged energy in the air, the weight of divided loyalties. Toward the back, she spotted Vincent and a few vineyard workers murmuring among themselves. Near the front, Peter Lawton sat with his face unreadable, watching intently.

Angela was already at the podium, her posture poised, exuding authority. She gazed over the crowd, her calm, composed expression one Sophie recognized as pure strategy. She was here to reassert her dominance, to remind Sonoma why so many had pledged their loyalty to her.

"Thank you all for coming," Angela began, her voice smooth and practiced. "I know there have been some... misunderstandings regarding my intentions for Sonoma. But, let me be clear—I have always had this town's best interests at heart. My investments in local businesses, my efforts to bring in tourism and revenue... they've all been for the good of Sonoma."

A murmur of agreement rippled through part of the crowd, and Sophie clenched her fists as Angela continued, her words oozing with practiced sincerity.

"But sometimes," Angela went on, letting her gaze sweep the room, "we have to make tough decisions. And sometimes, people cling to the past rather than embrace the future. The Cartwrights' vineyard is a beautiful piece of history, yes. But, history doesn't pay bills. It doesn't create jobs. I'm simply here to offer a solution that benefits us all."

Sophie glanced at James, seeing the sadness and frustration etched into his face as Angela dismissed his family's legacy with a casual, calculated smile.

Angela paused, then turned her gaze directly to James and Claire, her eyes sharp. "I understand the Cartwrights feel strongly about their land. But, let's not be distracted by rumors—accusations of bribery, of manipulation. Ask yourselves: does it make sense that I would need to resort to such tactics when all I've ever done is try to help this town?"

Sophie's anger boiled over. She stood, her voice clear and steady. "You may not need to, Angela, but that doesn't mean you haven't."

The room fell silent as every eye turned to her, some curious, others wary.

Angela's eyes narrowed, her composure slipping. "And who, exactly, are you to make these accusations?"

Sophie met her gaze, unflinching. "I'm someone who cares about the truth. You say you're here for Sonoma's good, but I've seen the lengths you're willing to go to get what you want—the payments to local businesses, the pressure on James, even the threats against anyone who dares to stand up to you."

Angela's mask cracked, her voice taking on an edge. "I'm not sure what you think you've 'uncovered,' Ms. Brooks, but you're an outsider. You don't understand how things work here."

Sophie held her ground. "I understand you're using money and fear to buy loyalty, turning people against James. And, I understand James is the last obstacle in your way."

A murmur rippled through the crowd. Sophie could sense that some of the townsfolk were questioning Angela's intentions.

Before she could continue, Peter Lawton shot to his feet, his voice booming. "Enough! These baseless accusations are slander, plain and simple. Angela has done more for this town than anyone else, and you—" he sneered at

Sophie, "you're just here to cause trouble, stirring up drama where there is none."

James stepped forward, his voice calm but resolute. "This isn't 'drama,' Peter. It's about protecting my family's land from someone who sees it as nothing more than a piece on her game board."

Angela's jaw clenched as she glared at James, her control slipping even further. "You're a fool, James. You're clinging to a relic and dragging this town down with you."

The tension was palpable, and a charged silence followed her words. Then, Claire stepped forward, her voice steady and resolute. "Our family built this vineyard from the ground up. It's not just a business—it's our history, our legacy. We're not going to let you take it away."

A few people in the crowd nodded, and Sophie saw the faintest crack in Angela's confidence. But, Angela's lips curled into a cold, calculated smile that sent a chill through Sophie.

"You'll regret this, James," she said, her voice laced with menace. "I promise you that."

The crowd dispersed slowly, the murmurs of heated discussion filling the square. Sophie, James, and Claire returned to the vineyard in silence, Angela's threat hanging heavily over them.

When they reached the house, Nate waited on the porch, his face pale. He waved them over, his expression troubled.

"What's wrong?" James asked, his voice low.

Nate glanced around, then whispered. "I didn't want to say this at the meeting, but I overheard something at the restaurant. Angela's lawyer, Peter, was talking with Greg Sanders, and they mentioned… blackmail."

Sophie's pulse quickened. "Blackmail? Against who?"

Nate looked at her, guilt shadowing his face. "Against me. And a few others who've supported the Cartwrights. Angela's been digging up dirt on anyone who might side with you, threatening to expose secrets, unless they back off."

Sophie's mind raced. Angela wasn't just bribing people. She was actively using blackmail to control anyone who opposed her. If they could find proof of this, it would be the final piece they needed to take her down.

"Nate, would you be willing to testify if we need you?" Sophie asked, her voice calm but urgent.

He hesitated, then nodded. "Yes. I'm tired of letting her bully this town."

James put a hand on Nate's shoulder, his gratitude evident. "Thank you, Nate. This means more to us than you know."

Sophie took a steadying breath. Angela's power was crumbling, and the town was finally seeing her for who she truly was. But, she knew Angela wouldn't go down without a fight.

With Nate's courage and the evidence they'd gathered, Sophie felt a renewed sense of hope. They would protect Cartwright Vineyard and stand up to Angela—no matter the cost.

CHAPTER 12
A DASH OF DECEPTION

THE MORNING after the town hall meeting, the Cartwright Vineyard was unusually quiet. Tension hung in the air, and Sophie could feel Angela's threat casting a shadow over them. They'd rattled her, exposing her tactics in front of the entire town, and Sophie knew Angela wouldn't let that go unanswered. But, they were too close to the truth to turn back now.

Sophie spent the morning with James and Claire, strategizing in the kitchen over cups of strong coffee. Nate had agreed to help them gather proof of Angela's blackmail, but testimony alone wouldn't be enough—they needed concrete evidence.

"I have a feeling Peter Lawton, her lawyer, is keeping records," Sophie said, her gaze flicking between James and Claire. "He's the one doing her 'damage control,' and if anyone has files on her payments or threats, it'll be him."

James nodded grimly. "Peter's as slippery as they come. I've dealt with him before, and he's always managed to twist things in Angela's favor."

"Where would he keep anything incriminating?" Claire asked, frowning. "He wouldn't leave it somewhere obvious."

Sophie thought for a moment. "If he's as meticulous as we think, he'd probably have a backup—maybe digital records on his computer."

Nate, who'd just arrived, joined the conversation, his jaw set. "If he has digital records, we might access them remotely. I know someone in town who's good with tech— if I explain the situation, he might help."

"Are you sure he'll be on board?" James asked, doubt in his voice.

Nate nodded. "He's not a fan of Angela or Peter. He's all about privacy and justice, and if he knows what's at stake, I think he'll help."

A surge of hope filled Sophie. This was their best chance at finding the evidence they needed, and she sensed they were finally close to unraveling Angela's hold over Sonoma.

THAT AFTERNOON, Sophie and Nate met with Danny, a young, tech-savvy local who ran a repair shop. Danny listened intently as they explained the situation, his sharp gaze focused as they described Angela's coercion and Peter's possible role.

"So, you think Peter has digital records of these payments and threats, and you want me to find a way in?" Danny asked, rubbing his chin.

"Yes," Sophie replied, steady. "We need concrete

evidence of Angela's manipulation. Witness statements won't be enough."

Danny considered this, then nodded, already typing on his laptop. "If Peter's security isn't too complex, I should be able to get in. Give me a day or so, and I'll let you know what I find."

Sophie left the shop feeling a renewed sense of purpose. With Danny's help, they might finally have the leverage they needed to expose Angela.

THAT NIGHT, Sophie couldn't shake the feeling of being watched. Ever since the town hall meeting, the sense of paranoia had crept over her, like Angela's presence was lingering in every shadow. She tried to focus on her notes, but the unease gnawed at her, making it hard to concentrate.

As she prepared to turn in for the night, she heard a noise outside—a soft rustling, like someone moving near the back of the guesthouse. Her heart leapt into her throat. She crept to the window, peering out into the darkness.

In the shadows, she recognized a figure in a dark coat. Her pulse quickened as she realized it was Peter Lawton, pacing near her door, glancing around as if ensuring no one was watching.

Sophie ducked out of sight, pressing her back against the wall to steady her breathing. Was he here to intimidate her, or to search for evidence?

Her phone lay just out of reach on the table. She held her breath as Peter moved closer to the door, the handle rattling slightly. After a tense moment, his footsteps receded, and she heard the soft start of a car engine. She peeked out to see his car disappearing into the night.

Shaken but resolved, she grabbed her phone and texted Nate and James.

Sophie: Peter was just here. He was outside my guest-house, trying to get in.

Nate: What? Are you okay?

Sophie: I'm fine. But it's clear he's getting desperate. He must know we're close.

JAMES: IF PETER'S SHOWING UP AT YOUR PLACE, ANGELA'S RUNNING OUT OF PATIENCE.

They agreed to meet at the main house the next morning to plan their next move. That night, Sophie lay wide awake, certain now that Peter held the key to exposing Angela's control over the town.

THE NEXT MORNING, Danny called, his voice charged with excitement. "Sophie, you're going to want to see this. I got into Peter's files."

Sophie's heart pounded. "Did you find anything?"

"Oh, I found plenty," Danny replied. "He's kept records of every payment Angela's made to her 'allies'— business owners, vineyard workers, even some city officials. There are emails between him and Angela discussing ways to pressure James into selling."

Sophie could hardly believe it. This was the proof they'd been searching for, solid evidence of Angela's manipulation and coercion.

"Can you print the files?" she asked, urgency clear in her voice.

"Already on it," Danny replied. "Just promise me you'll be careful. Angela's not going to like this."

"Don't worry," Sophie said, a steely determination in her tone. "We'll handle it."

ARMED WITH THE PRINTED FILES, Sophie, James, Claire, and Nate made their way to Angela's estate. Standing on her doorstep, Sophie felt the weight of the moment—the culmination of weeks of threats, investigation, and hidden alliances.

Angela opened the door, her face stony. "What do you want?"

James stepped forward, his expression fierce but calm. "We know what you've been doing, Angela. And, we have the proof."

He held up the files, and Angela's face paled as she recognized them. For a moment, her mask of composure slipped, revealing a flash of panic, before she quickly regained control.

"This is absurd," she scoffed, her voice icy. "You think you can threaten me with a few pieces of paper? No one will believe you."

Sophie stepped forward, her voice steady. "These documents show every payment you've made, every bribe, every piece of blackmail. You've been manipulating this town to create your personal empire. But it ends here."

Angela's eyes narrowed, fury simmering beneath her mask. "You think you've won? I still have options."

James's steady voice cut through the tension. "No, Angela. You're done here."

For a tense moment, Angela and James locked eyes, the bitterness and history between them hanging heavy in the air. Then, without another word, Angela slammed the door, her footsteps echoing as she stormed away.

Sophie let out a shaky breath, adrenaline coursing through her. They'd done it. They'd confronted Angela, and now they had the evidence to back up their claims.

But the victory was short-lived. Two nights later, James's lifeless body was found at the foot of the vineyard's steps.

OVER THE FOLLOWING DAYS, news of Angela's manipulation swept through Sonoma. The town council launched an investigation, and Angela's former supporters quickly distanced themselves, appalled by her deception. Sonoma's loyalty shifted, with locals rallying around James and the Cartwright Vineyard, determined to preserve their town's legacy.

One evening, as Sophie sat on the guesthouse porch watching the sunset over the vineyard, her phone buzzed with a message from Oliver.

> Oliver: Looks like you cracked the case, detective! Proud of you.

Sophie smiled, warmth spreading through her. She'd come to Sonoma to write but had found something deeper —a community worth fighting for and a legacy worth preserving.

As she gazed out over the vineyard, the rows of vines bathed in soft twilight, a sense of peace settled over her. The threats, tension, and danger were finally behind her. In their place was a story she'd carry forever—a reminder of courage, resilience, and the power of truth.

CHAPTER 13
HARVESTING DOUBT

SOPHIE COULDN'T SHAKE the unease that had settled over her since Peter's bold, late-night appearance outside her guesthouse. His attempt at intimidation was explicit confirmation of what she'd feared—Angela and her allies were out of options. But, their desperation only fueled Sophie's resolve. She was closing in on something, and desperation led to mistakes. Now, she just had to catch one.

After a quick breakfast, she returned to the Cartwright main house, determined to comb through James's records once more. A nagging feeling told her she'd missed something, perhaps a hidden thread that would unravel Angela's next move. Her mind drifted to her recent conversations with Vincent and the faint sense that not all secrets were Angela's alone.

Claire met her at the door, her smile a little forced, her face shadowed with exhaustion. It seemed the recent confrontations had taken a toll, yet Sophie noticed an additional tension in her friend's expression, something she couldn't quite place.

"Sophie," Claire said, attempting a smile. "Ready to dive back into the ledgers? I swear I'll be seeing columns and invoices in my sleep."

Sophie returned the smile but kept her mind alert. If Claire was entangled in Angela's scheme, she'd need to tread carefully to uncover the truth without arousing suspicion.

They spent hours sifting through James's records in the study. Sophie carefully examined each ledger and invoice, noting the ongoing struggle James had faced to keep the vineyard financially viable. But one ledger stood out—a small, leather-bound book that had been set apart, as though James didn't want it mixed in with the primary records.

As Sophie flipped through the pages, she noticed unusual labels like "consultation fee" and "miscellaneous expense," along with checks signed by James but made out to "C. Cartwright"—Claire. Her heart skipped a beat as she examined the amounts. They weren't exorbitant, but they were significant enough to raise questions. If the payments were innocent, why had James been so secretive about them?

Sophie's mind raced, piecing together possibilities. Was it possible that Claire had been receiving these payments for something beyond James's knowledge? Or could Angela have exploited Claire? She fought to keep her expression neutral as she continued her search, glancing at Claire from the corner of her eye. If these payments were tied to Claire, then perhaps the threat to the vineyard wasn't just coming from outsiders.

"What's that you're looking at?" Claire asked, breaking Sophie's concentration.

"Oh, just one of the older ledgers," Sophie replied casually, though her thoughts spun. "I think I'm starting to see where some of the vineyard's financial strain was coming from."

Claire sighed. "I'm not surprised. Uncle James struggled with finances for years, but he was too proud to let anyone help. It's probably why he didn't tell me about the debts until it was nearly too late."

Sophie noted the honesty in Claire's tone but couldn't shake her growing suspicion. If Claire didn't know the full extent of James's financial strain, why had there been payments in her name? And if she did... why had she kept it from Sophie?

After another hour of sifting through records in silence, Sophie found an envelope tucked into the back of the leather ledger, marked with a single word: Confidential. Her pulse quickened as she discreetly opened it. Inside was a single check, made out to "C. Cartwright" for a considerable sum, but this time, the signature wasn't James's. It was barely legible, but after a moment, Sophie recognized it: Angela Mason.

The implications hit her hard. Angela had paid Claire directly. Sophie held up the check. "This isn't just a payment. It's a statement. Angela wanted Claire to think she owed her, to feel trapped by this so-called generosity."

Claire's voice was barely a whisper. "I didn't want to take it, but I thought I had no choice."

This could mean one of two things—either Claire had turned to Angela for help behind James's back, or Angela had somehow manipulated Claire into her scheme to gain control of the vineyard.

Sophie's heart raced. Could Claire really be involved? Or was she an unwitting pawn, pulled into Angela's influence without knowing the full picture? Sophie had to be cautious. Confronting Claire outright could risk their friendship—or worse, expose Claire's vulnerabilities to Angela's allies.

BACK AT HER GUESTHOUSE, Sophie sat at her desk, staring at the check. She needed perspective, someone she could trust who would give her unbiased advice. She picked up her phone and texted Oliver.

> Sophie: Hey, I need a sounding board. This investigation's getting messier than I expected.

Oliver replied almost immediately.

> Oliver: Messy is your specialty. Hit me with it.

> Sophie: Found a check from Angela to Claire. Could mean Claire's working with Angela or... maybe she's trapped in this somehow.

> Oliver: Whoa. So you're saying Claire might be a double agent? Didn't see that one coming.

> Sophie: It doesn't add up. Claire's been nothing but supportive. I can't believe she'd betray her family after everything that's happened.

> Oliver: Hmm. Think about it — Angela's good at turning people's weaknesses into leverage. What if Claire needed help, or Angela had dirt on her?

Sophie's mind churned as she read his response. Angela was indeed a master at exploiting vulnerabilities. If Claire was compromised, it would explain her secrecy and reluctance to share certain details.

> Sophie: That makes sense. I need to ask her directly, but if I'm wrong...

> Oliver: Then she'll understand that you're looking for the truth. If she's innocent, she won't hold it against you. Go with your gut, Soph. It hasn't let you down yet.

Sophie felt a wave of gratitude. Oliver's confidence in her was just what she needed to push through her hesitation. She would confront Claire, but she'd do it gently, understanding that Claire might be as much a victim as anyone else.

> Sophie: Thanks, Oliver. You're my rock.

> Oliver: All in a day's work for your loyal Watson. Now go crack this case.

Sophie put her phone down, her resolve steadying. Tomorrow, she'd confront Claire, balancing her loyalty with the need for the truth. She felt the weight of her next steps settle over her, a reminder that she was no longer a mere observer—she was in the middle of this story, fighting to preserve a legacy.

As Sophie prepared for bed, she knew that the truth was close, perhaps closer than ever before. And, she was ready to face it, no matter what it revealed about the people she thought she knew.

CHAPTER 14
WINE AND WHISPERS

SOPHIE WOKE with a knot of anxiety twisting in her stomach. Today, she would confront Claire about the check from Angela. Despite her determination to uncover the truth, she dreaded what she might find. If Claire was innocent, she deserved the chance to explain. But if not…

After a quick breakfast, Sophie walked to the main house, rehearsing how she'd bring up the check without accusations. She found Claire outside, hunched over a small herb garden near the kitchen. She glanced up as Sophie approached, her smile tired.

"Hey, Sophie," Claire greeted, brushing a strand of hair back. "Couldn't stay away from the vineyard, huh?"

Sophie managed a smile, though her heart raced. "Actually, there's something I need to talk to you about. It's… important."

Claire straightened, her expression shifting to concern. "Is everything okay?"

Sophie took a deep breath, steadying herself. "I found

something yesterday while going through James's ledgers. A check from Angela, made out to you."

For a moment, Claire's face froze, her expression carefully controlled, but Sophie saw the flicker of something— fear, guilt, or perhaps both.

"Angela paid me?" Claire's voice was barely above a whisper.

"Yes," Sophie replied, watching her closely. "It wasn't a small amount. I thought... maybe you could tell me what it was for?"

Claire's gaze dropped to the ground, her shoulders slumping. She sighed heavily, then motioned for Sophie to follow. They walked in silence to a secluded bench beneath the old oaks, each step tightening the dread coiling in Sophie's stomach. Once they were seated, Claire took a deep breath, looking out across the vineyard with a distant, haunted expression.

"About a year ago, Angela approached me with an offer," Claire began, her voice thick with bitterness. "She said she knew about Uncle James's financial troubles and wanted to 'help'—on her terms, of course. She offered me money to keep the vineyard afloat. Said it would 'ease James's burden,' at least for a while."

Sophie's mind raced. "But, Angela wouldn't help out of kindness. What did she want in return?"

Claire pressed her lips into a thin line. "Information. She asked me to update her on Uncle James's plans— whether he was considering selling, talking to other buyers. At first, I thought she just wanted to be prepared. But over time, it was clear she was trying to control him, wear him down until he'd have no choice but to sell."

Sophie's heart sank. The weight of Claire's words hit

her hard. "Why didn't you tell James? Or refuse Angela's money?"

Claire's voice filled with shame. "I refused, at first. But, she kept pressuring me. She said if I didn't cooperate, she'd expose our debts to the town—make it impossible for us to get help, maybe even drive us out." Her gaze dropped. "I thought I could handle it. I thought I was helping."

Sophie felt a flash of anger on Claire's behalf. "That's exactly what people like her do," she murmured, her voice hardening. "They make you feel helpless, turn loyalty against you."

Claire's eyes met hers, and Sophie hesitated before continuing, her voice lower. "Back in Oregon, I trusted someone like her. My ex. He brushed off my concerns, made deals behind my back, cut me out until I'd lost everything I'd built. I won't stand by and watch you go through the same thing."

Claire gave a shaky nod, gratitude mingling with relief in her eyes. "Then, let's make sure she doesn't win."

Sophie thought back to the town hall, the tension between James and Angela. Claire, despite her guilt, had been an unwilling pawn in Angela's manipulation. She'd twisted Claire's loyalty, used it to weaken the Cartwrights and the vineyard.

"Claire," Sophie said gently, "why didn't you confide in James? He would have understood."

Claire's voice broke. "I was ashamed. And, after Uncle James died... I felt like I'd failed him. Like I'd let her win."

Sophie reached over, resting a hand on her shoulder. "Angela is ruthless, and she knew how to manipulate you. You were trying to protect what he loved."

A flicker of hope stirred in Claire's eyes. "I wish I'd been strong enough to stand up to her sooner. Maybe if I had, he'd still be here."

The two sat in silence, the weight of Claire's confession settling over them. Sophie saw the toll Angela's control had taken on her friend, eroding her confidence and leaving her trapped in guilt.

"Claire," Sophie said gently, "you said Angela used this against you. Did she ever threaten you outright?"

Claire nodded slowly. "A few times, she hinted that if I didn't cooperate, she'd ruin my reputation. I didn't know if she'd do it, but I couldn't risk it. So, I stayed quiet."

Sophie's jaw tightened. Angela's hold on Claire was even more sinister than she'd imagined. But now that they knew the truth, they could turn the tables.

"We can use this, Claire," Sophie said, her voice steady. "Angela manipulated you, and we have the proof. If we confront her with it, it might be enough to make her back down."

A glimmer of hope sparked in Claire's eyes, though she remained cautious. "But Angela's powerful, Sophie. She won't go down without a fight."

"Then, we'll be ready. We have allies, Claire. Nate, the town, and now… the truth."

Claire took a deep breath, nodding as a new resolve took root. "Thank you, Sophie. I don't know what I would've done without you."

They shared a moment of quiet solidarity, united by a common purpose. For the first time, Sophie felt they had a real chance of breaking Angela's hold over the vineyard.

THAT EVENING, Sophie and Claire met Nate and headed to Angela's estate. The sun was setting, casting long shadows across the hills as they approached the grand front door. Sophie could feel the tension, but her determination held firm. They wouldn't leave until Angela answered for what she'd done.

Angela opened the door, her expression icy as she took in the three of them standing before her.

"Can I help you?" she asked, her voice cool, but her eyes were wary.

"Yes," Sophie replied, holding up the check Angela had made out to Claire. "We need to talk about your... financial involvement with Claire."

Angela's mask faltered, her eyes flashing with irritation. "I don't know what you're talking about."

Sophie stepped forward. "Oh, I think you do. You've been manipulating Claire, using her loyalty to feed you information about James and the vineyard. You gave this check to Claire knowing she'd never cash it. But the real control wasn't in the money. It was in the fear you created-the fear of what you'd do if she didn't cooperate. Your control ends here."

Angela's face hardened, and for a moment, her composure slipped, revealing cold fury. "You think you can come here with wild accusations?"

"Save it, Angela," Claire said, her voice stronger than Sophie had ever heard it. "I know what you did. You twisted my loyalty, used me to get to Uncle James. I'm done letting you use me."

Angela's expression turned venomous. "You think you can threaten me? I could ruin all of you with one phone call."

Sophie met her gaze, unfazed. "Do what you need to. But, the truth has a way of surfacing, Angela. If you keep pushing, Sonoma will know exactly who you are."

For a moment, Angela seemed to waver, her control slipping as she took in the strength in Sophie's eyes. But, she quickly straightened, her expression hardening.

"This isn't over," she hissed, her voice like ice. "You have no idea what you're up against."

Without another word, she turned and slammed the door, leaving them in the cool evening air.

Sophie let out a slow breath, feeling the tension drain from her. They hadn't forced a confession, but they'd made an impact. Angela knew they weren't backing down, and that was enough to keep her off-balance.

As they walked back to the car, Claire reached for Sophie's hand, giving it a grateful squeeze. "Thank you, Sophie. For everything."

Sophie smiled. The fight wasn't over, but they were closer than ever to exposing the truth. Together, they would see this through to the end.

CHAPTER 15
A TOAST TO ALLIES

AFTER THE TENSE confrontation with Angela, Sophie felt both exhilarated and drained. Angela's reaction had confirmed her suspicions, but they were still far from securing the vineyard's future. They'd rattled Angela, but her parting words made it clear that she wouldn't go down without a fight.

That evening, Sophie headed to Nate's restaurant, hoping he might offer advice on their next move. Since she'd arrived in Sonoma, Nate had become more than just an ally—he was a source of support, and his grounded perspective helped balance her own swirling thoughts. Tonight, she felt the weight of Angela's threats pressing down on her, and Nate's steady presence was exactly what she needed.

The restaurant was quieting down for the night, and Nate was at the bar, wiping down glasses when he spotted her. He smiled, setting aside his cloth. "Sophie, hey! Perfect timing—I was just about to close up. Join me for a drink?"

Sophie returned his smile, a sense of relief washing over her. "I'd love that. I think we could both use one after the past few days."

They settled at a small table near the bar, and Nate poured two glasses of deep red wine from a local vineyard. The wine's warm, earthy aroma filled the air, and Sophie took a grateful sip. For a moment, they sat in companionable silence, the quiet of the empty restaurant a welcome reprieve.

"So," Nate said finally, setting down his glass. "How did it go with Angela?"

Sophie sighed. "Better than I expected, but not enough. We confronted her, laid everything out, but she didn't exactly confess. If anything, I think we just made her more determined to push back."

Nate nodded, his gaze thoughtful. "That sounds like Angela. She's never been one to back down, especially when someone challenges her."

Sophie looked down at her glass, the question that had been gnawing at her finally surfacing. "Nate, why do you think she's so fixated on the Cartwright Vineyard? I know it's about power and legacy, but this feels more personal. Like it's more than just business."

Nate leaned back, his gaze growing reflective. "You're right—it is personal. The Masons and the Cartwrights have a long history, and it hasn't always been friendly. Angela's family has always been ambitious, but they've resented that the Cartwrights held a special place in Sonoma's history. I think, to Angela, owning that vineyard would be rewriting the town's legacy to favor her family."

Sophie absorbed his words, realizing that the vineyard wasn't just valuable land. It was a symbol, a testament to the Cartwright legacy. Angela didn't just want the property—she wanted to erase the Cartwrights' influence and claim Sonoma for herself.

"She's ruthless," Sophie murmured, shaking her head. "She's willing to ruin anyone who stands in her way, even if it damages her own family's reputation."

"That's exactly what makes her dangerous," Nate agreed. "Angela doesn't see people as people. To her, they're tools, obstacles, or assets. And, she's willing to use any means necessary to get what she wants."

Sophie looked at Nate, sensing a depth of understanding in his words. "Did you ever have to deal with her directly?"

Nate hesitated, his gaze growing distant. "Angela approached me a few years back. She wanted me to join her campaign to 'modernize' Sonoma, expand the town's footprint, draw in more tourism. She said my restaurant would be a 'cornerstone' in her vision."

Sophie raised an eyebrow, feeling a pang of empathy. "What did you say?"

"I told her no," Nate replied, his voice carrying a note of defiance. "I moved here to escape all that, to build something real. The last thing I wanted was to turn this place into another tourist trap. But, Angela didn't take kindly to that answer. She started dropping hints, suggesting that if I didn't get on board, I'd be left out of future 'opportunities.'"

Sophie's heart tightened with a mix of admiration and sympathy. She knew that kind of pressure all too well—Angela's tactics were as manipulative as they were effective, leaving fractured loyalties and resentment in her wake.

"Do you regret it?" she asked softly. "Saying no to her?"

Nate shook his head, his expression resolute. "Not for a second. This place, this community… it's worth fighting for. I'd rather struggle to keep my independence than sell out to someone like Angela."

Sophie felt a surge of respect for him. He was more than an ally—he understood what it meant to stand up for what mattered, even when it came at a cost. She realized then that his support meant more than she'd admitted to herself.

"Nate," she began, her voice softening, "I'm not sure I would've made it this far without you. You've made Sonoma feel like home."

He looked at her, his expression softening in response. "Sophie, you've done more for this town in a few weeks than most people do in years. You've uncovered things that people were too afraid to confront. And, you're giving the Cartwrights a real chance to save their legacy."

They held each other's gaze, a quiet intensity settling between them. Sophie felt her cheeks warm as she realized the depth of her feelings—not just for the vineyard, but for Nate himself.

He cleared his throat, breaking the silence. "What's the next move?"

Sophie took a deep breath, refocusing. "We need more evidence. We're close, but without something concrete, Angela could still twist things and turn the town against the Cartwrights. Claire mentioned that James might have kept letters or documents we haven't found yet."

Nate's gaze sharpened. "Then, we'll find them. If James left anything behind, we'll make sure they comes to light."

They now had a plan, and with Nate's help, they stood a real chance of exposing Angela's schemes and protecting the vineyard.

They finished their wine in a comfortable silence, an unspoken understanding strengthening the connection between them. For the first time since arriving in Sonoma, Sophie felt she was exactly where she was meant to be.

THE NEXT MORNING, Sophie returned to the Cartwright main house, determined to search every corner for any documents James might have left behind. Claire met her at the door, her expression more hopeful than it had been in days.

"Nate told me you're looking for more documents," Claire said, leading her inside. "I actually remembered something this morning. Uncle James used to keep a small safe in his office—he said it was for 'important things.' I don't know if there's anything relevant in there, but it's worth a look."

Sophie's heart leapt. A safe could be exactly what they needed. "Do you know the combination?"

Claire nodded, excitement sparking in her eyes. "Yes, I remember it. Let's check."

In James's office, Claire led her to a low cabinet tucked behind the desk. She opened it, revealing a small, sturdy safe. With steady hands, Claire turned the dial, her fingers moving confidently over the familiar numbers.

The safe door clicked open, and Claire pulled out a small stack of papers. She handed them to Sophie, her face tense with anticipation.

Sophie carefully flipped through the documents. Most were routine property deeds, tax returns, and legal agreements. But near the bottom, she found a letter—its paper yellowed, its edges worn.

The letter was addressed to James from a friend named Thomas Caldwell, who'd left Sonoma years ago. As Sophie read, her pulse quickened.

In the letter, Thomas mentioned that he'd overheard Angela's father discussing a "contingency plan" to take over the Cartwright Vineyard if it ever fell into financial trouble. The tone suggested something underhanded, a potential deal to force the Cartwrights out if they hit hard times.

Sophie looked at Claire, her excitement building. "This could be it, Claire. It's not hard evidence, but it's something. If we can tie this to Angela's recent actions, we might prove that her family's been plotting this for years."

Claire's eyes brightened, determination flaring. "Then, let's do it. Let's show everyone who Angela really is."

As Sophie walked back to her guesthouse, her phone buzzed with a message from Nate.

> Nate: How's the investigation, Detective?
> Found anything juicy?

Sophie grinned, typing back quickly.

Sophie: Yes! We found an old letter hinting that Angela's family has been planning this takeover for years. It's not everything, but it's a start.

Nate: Impressive, Sherlock. You know, if you ever get tired of the writing gig, you'd make one heck of an investigator.

Sophie laughed softly, warmth spreading through her. She'd come to Sonoma feeling lost, unsure of her purpose. But now, she had allies beside her and a community worth fighting for.

Sophie: Thanks, Nate. Couldn't have done any of this without you.

Nate: Anytime. Now go solve this thing. Sonoma's counting on you.

With Nate's encouragement and the discovery of the letter, Sophie's confidence grew. Angela's grip on Sonoma was loosening, and with a little more digging, they'd have what they needed to expose her.

She walked through the vineyard, sunlight casting warm shadows over the rows of vines. This was more than just solving a mystery—it was about preserving the soul of Sonoma and finding a place to call her own.

And, she was ready for whatever lay ahead.

CHAPTER 16
THE VINTAGE OF DECEIT

SOPHIE RETURNED to the Cartwright main house early the next morning, her mind racing with the possibility that they might finally be close to exposing Angela's twisted schemes. The letter from James's friend had hinted at a long-standing plan by Angela's family to seize control of Cartwright Vineyard. Now, with the mounting evidence, Sophie felt closer than ever to piecing together the full picture.

Claire was waiting for her in the study, a nervous energy radiating from her as they reviewed the documents from James's safe one more time. "Sophie, do you really think this letter could help us?" she asked, hope in her voice but doubt in her eyes.

"It's a start," Sophie replied, giving her friend a reassuring smile. "If we can find recent documents linking Angela to the vineyard's financial troubles, we might prove she was actively trying to sabotage James. And, if she's been blackmailing you, there might be evidence of that here, too."

They combed through the papers, searching for anything that could confirm their suspicions. Sophie's eyes caught a small envelope tucked between old invoices, almost hidden, marked with a single word: **Confidential**.

Her heart pounded as she opened the envelope, carefully unfolding the letter inside. She recognized the slanted, familiar handwriting instantly—Angela's. Addressed to Claire, the letter was a veiled threat, warning that if Claire didn't cooperate by feeding Angela information, her family's reputation—and the vineyard—would suffer. Angela alluded to debts, hinted at past mistakes, and listed "unfortunate decisions" that could be made public. She even referenced personal details about Claire's life, details that clearly weren't meant to see daylight.

Sophie felt her stomach churn as she read. This was it. Angela had used blackmail to force Claire into betraying her own family, exploiting her loyalty to the vineyard.

"Claire…" Sophie looked up, her face a mix of sympathy and anger. "This letter—Angela really did blackmail you, didn't she?"

Claire's hands shook as she held the letter. "I never thought she'd put this in writing. She must have been overconfident. She probably believed no one would look through James's old invoices."

Sophie frowned. "Or maybe she didn't think anyone would question her. Angela's strength has always been intimidation. She didn't expect us to dig."

Sophie placed a comforting hand on Claire's shoulder. "Angela probably didn't expect anyone to find this. But now that we have it, we have proof. She is manipulating you, Claire. You don't have to be afraid of her anymore."

Claire looked up, a glimmer of relief breaking through

her despair. "Do you really think this will be enough to expose her?"

"It's a strong piece of evidence," Sophie said firmly. "Combined with the other documents, we're building a clear picture of what Angela's been doing. She's systematically isolated you and tried to force James into selling. She's used every tactic—blackmail, manipulation, financial pressure."

Sophie spread the documents on the table. "Angela didn't just want the vineyard. She wanted control. Control over the town, its economy, its people. By taking the vineyard, she could cement her power."

Claire nodded slowly. "And she knew James wouldn't back down. That's why she had to remove him."

Claire gripped the letter, her knuckles white. "I can't believe I let her control me like this. I should have seen it sooner."

"You're not to blame," Sophie said. "Angela knew exactly how to get to you. But now, you have the power to stop her. We just need to decide how to use this."

They sat in silence, the weight of their discovery settling over them. Sophie knew that confronting Angela wouldn't be easy—her connections and influence ran deep. But, this letter was a turning point, a concrete piece of evidence they could use to bring Angela's schemes to light.

FEELING the impact of their discovery, Sophie and Claire met Nate at his restaurant to share the news. Nate was closing up for the afternoon when they arrived, his welcoming smile fading to seriousness as he saw the intensity on their faces.

"What's going on?" he asked, motioning for them to sit at a quiet table in the back.

Sophie took a steadying breath, laying the letter out on the table. "We found proof, Nate. Angela's been blackmailing Claire to gain control of the vineyard."

Nate's eyes widened as he read the letter, his shock quickly replaced by anger. "This is… despicable. Angela's always been ruthless, but this? Blackmailing her own family?"

Claire nodded, her voice trembling. "She's been holding this over my head for months, threatening to ruin our reputation if I didn't cooperate. I thought I could handle it, that I could keep her at arm's length… but she just kept pushing, tightening her grip."

Nate reached across the table, resting a reassuring hand on Claire's. "You're not alone anymore, Claire. We're in this together."

Sophie's resolve strengthened. "If we can find just a bit more—something that directly links Angela's threats to her attempts to buy the vineyard—we'll have everything we need to expose her."

Nate's face hardened. "There's one person who might help us connect those dots: Peter Lawton. Angela's lawyer has been her right-hand man through all of this. He's cunning, but he's arrogant. I'd bet he has records of every shady deal she's made."

Sophie's heart raced at the idea. "If we could access his files, we might find more proof of Angela's manipulation. But how? There's no way he'd let us just walk into his office and start digging around."

Nate's lips curved into a mischievous smile. "Peter's a regular at a poker game I host once a month. Tonight's the night. When he's focused on winning, he won't notice if someone slips away to do a little 'research.'"

Sophie felt a thrill of anticipation. "Let's do it."

THAT EVENING, Sophie and Nate arrived at the poker game in the back room of Nate's restaurant. The room was filled with familiar faces, including Peter Lawton, who sat confidently at the table, drink in hand, basking in his usual air of self-assurance. Sophie watched him closely, noting the way he casually commanded the room.

Once the game got underway, Sophie excused herself, slipping quietly out of the room. Following Nate's plan, she made her way to Peter's office in a nearby suite he rented. Using the spare key Nate had secured, she unlocked the door and stepped inside, her pulse hammering.

Her phone's flashlight illuminated Peter's desk, a sleek space lined with polished wood and meticulously stacked files. She moved quickly, sifting through folders and flipping through papers, her fingers trembling as she searched for anything incriminating.

At last, she found a folder labeled "Cartwright Acquisition." Her pulse quickened as she opened it, scanning the documents. Within moments, she found a series of emails and letters exchanged between Peter and Angela. Each one detailed her plans for the vineyard—her financial offers, her backup schemes, and the subtle pressure she'd exerted on the community to isolate James.

But, one email, recent and bold, caught her eye. In it, Angela instructed Peter to "increase the pressure" on Claire, referencing her "financial vulnerabilities." The language was cryptic but unmistakable—Peter had been actively assisting Angela in her attempts to coerce Claire into compliance.

Sophie photographed the documents, her hands steadying as she captured each page. This was the proof they needed. Angela had enlisted Peter to blackmail Claire, exploiting her financial insecurities to tighten her grip on the vineyard. With this, they could finally confront Angela publicly.

Footsteps echoed outside the door, and Sophie slipped out, returning to the poker game just as Peter smirked over a winning hand. She exchanged a subtle nod with Nate, signaling her success.

LATER THAT NIGHT, Sophie, Nate, and Claire gathered at the guesthouse, the weight of their discovery filling the room as they reviewed the evidence.

"We have everything we need," Sophie said, her voice brimming with determination. "Angela's threats to Claire, her schemes to manipulate the town, and now proof that Peter was her accomplice. This isn't just unethical—it's criminal."

Nate nodded, his face set. "We'll take it to the town council. And, if they're willing, we'll bring it to the authorities. Angela's influence runs deep, but with evidence like this, she won't be able to dodge the consequences."

Claire looked at the stack of papers, relief and disbelief

mingling in her eyes. "I can't believe it's almost over... or that we have a real shot at stopping her."

Sophie placed a steadying hand on her shoulder. "We're ready, Claire. Tomorrow, we'll confront Angela head-on. This ends now."

As they finalized their plan, Sophie felt a deep sense of purpose settle within her. The investigation had tested her courage and resilience, but now, with her friends beside her, she was ready to bring everything to light.

Tomorrow, they would expose Angela—and reclaim the Cartwright legacy.

CHAPTER 17
FERMENTING FEAR

THE SUN HAD BARELY RISEN when Sophie was jolted awake by insistent pounding on her guesthouse door. She shot up, her heart racing as last night's events flooded back: the secret poker game, her tense search of Peter's office, and the damning evidence she'd uncovered linking Angela to the blackmail.

She threw on a sweater, hurried to the door, and opened it to find Nate, his face etched with worry.

"Sophie," he said, his voice urgent. "Something happened at the vineyard last night."

Her stomach dropped. "What do you mean? Is Claire okay?"

"Claire's fine," he assured her, though the tension in his eyes didn't ease. "But, someone vandalized the main house—broken windows, graffiti... and they left a message on the door."

Sophie's pulse quickened as she grabbed her coat and followed Nate into the chilly morning air. As they hurried toward the main house, questions raced through her mind. Who would go to such lengths to intimidate them? What kind of message had they left?

When they arrived, Nate hadn't exaggerated. One of the front windows was shattered, jagged shards glittering across the ground. On the door, fresh, red letters stood stark against the wood:

"STOP NOW OR ELSE."

Claire was standing on the porch, arms wrapped around herself as she stared at the words. She turned to Sophie, her face pale.

"Sophie… who would do this?" she whispered, her voice trembling.

Sophie took a deep breath, suppressing her own surge of anger. "I think we both know who's behind this. Angela's feeling the pressure, and she's getting desperate."

Claire nodded, her eyes wide. "But, to do something so… so public? Doesn't she realize this makes her look even more guilty?"

"Maybe," Nate said grimly, "but Angela's not used to losing. She's hoping this will scare you into backing off. When someone like her feels cornered, that's when they're the most dangerous."

Sophie clenched her fists, her resolve hardening. Angela's scare tactics only steeled her determination. "We're not backing down," she said, meeting Claire's gaze. "If anything, this just proves we're getting closer."

Claire straightened, her shoulders squaring. "You're right. We've come too far to stop now."

But, as they stood together, surveying the damage, Sophie felt a prickle of unease. She glanced around, her gaze sweeping over the rows of vines shrouded in morning mist. Was Angela lurking somewhere nearby, watching to see if her threat had landed?

Sophie pushed down the feeling. They had a plan, and they wouldn't let Angela derail it now.

As they cleaned up the damage, a familiar figure strode up the path toward the house. Sheriff Davis, his expression hard, took in the scene with a practiced eye, his gaze lingering on the broken window and the graffiti on the door.

"What happened here?" he asked brusquely.

Sophie exchanged a look with Claire before stepping forward. "Someone broke in last night. They vandalized the place and left a message—'Stop now or else.' We think Angela's behind it."

The sheriff raised an eyebrow. "That's a serious accusation. Do you have any proof?"

Sophie fought to keep her frustration in check. The sheriff had been wary of her investigation from the start, and she could sense his skepticism.

"We have evidence," she replied, keeping her voice calm. "Angela's been blackmailing Claire, using threats to manipulate her into helping with her plan to take over the vineyard. And last night, I found documents in Peter Lawton's office confirming Angela's involvement."

The sheriff's frown deepened as he looked from Sophie

to Claire and then to Nate. "You're telling me you uncovered all this on your own?"

Sophie nodded, her gaze steady. "We have a folder full
of documents linking Angela to the blackmail and coercion. I'd be happy to show you everything."

The sheriff studied her for a moment before giving a
reluctant nod. "Alright. Bring what you have to the station
later today, and we'll take a look. But, I'll warn you—
Angela has a lot of influence around here. If you're wrong
about this, it could mean trouble for all of you."

Sophie's jaw tightened. "We understand the risks, Sheriff. But we also know that Angela's actions have gone
unchecked for too long. It's time someone stood up to
her."

The sheriff gave her a searching look, then nodded. "I'll
expect you at the station by noon. In the meantime, keep
your guard up. Whoever did this might not be finished
yet."

As he left, Sophie felt a flicker of satisfaction. They
finally had the sheriff's attention, and with any luck, they
could use the evidence they'd gathered to turn the tide.

BACK AT HER GUESTHOUSE, Sophie carefully organized the
documents she'd collected, preparing them for her
meeting with the sheriff. The folder was full—Angela's
letters, Peter's emails, financial records—all meticulously
cataloged, forming a damning picture of Angela's
schemes. She knew this was their best chance to expose
Angela and end her hold over Sonoma once and for all.

As she finished, her phone buzzed with a message from an unknown number. Frowning, she opened the text:

"You're making a mistake. Stop now, or you'll regret it."

A chill ran down her spine. The message was blunt, its menace unmistakable. She knew without a doubt that it was from someone connected to Angela.

Steeling herself, Sophie saved the message and forwarded it to both Nate and Claire. They needed to be on high alert.

Nate responded immediately.

> Nate: That's it, Sophie. We're sticking together until this is over. I don't like the idea of you being alone right now.

> Claire: Please be careful, Sophie. We're almost there. Don't let them scare you.

Sophie took a deep breath, feeling a surge of gratitude for their support. She wasn't facing this alone and that gave her strength.

AT NOON, Sophie, Nate, and Claire arrived at the sheriff's station, the weight of their mission pressing down on them. Sheriff Davis met them in his office, his expression unreadable as he motioned for them to sit.

Sophie placed the folder on his desk and watched as he opened it, flipping through the documents with growing intensity. The room was silent as the sheriff examined each page, his eyes narrowing at the extent of Angela's manipulation.

Finally, he closed the folder, looking up with a hard expression. "This... this is serious. If these documents hold up, Angela Mason has been using threats and coercion to control not just the Cartwrights, but others in the community, too."

Sophie nodded, her heart pounding. "We believe she was behind the vandalism this morning. And, I received a threatening message just a few hours ago, warning me to drop the investigation."

The sheriff's gaze sharpened. "Angela's influence has kept many people silent. But, with this... we can finally hold her accountable. I'll need to question her and Peter, and verify the authenticity of these documents. But, you may have just tipped the scales."

A surge of relief washed over Sophie. They'd done it. They'd brought the evidence to light, and the sheriff was taking it seriously.

"Thank you, Sheriff," she said, her voice full of gratitude. "We just want to protect the Cartwrights and the community from any more of Angela's schemes."

The sheriff nodded, his expression firm. "We'll proceed, but you need to be cautious. If Angela feels cornered, she could become even more dangerous."

Sophie glanced at Nate and Claire, sensing their shared resolve. They understood the risks, but they were ready to face whatever came next.

As THEY RETURNED to the guesthouse, Sophie felt a surge of accomplishment tempered by a lingering unease. The sheriff's warning echoed in her mind—Angela was dangerous, and they'd just forced her into a corner.

They'd barely settled in when a loud crash shattered the quiet evening. Sophie rushed outside, her heart pounding. She saw smoke rising from the barn near the vineyard's main house.

Claire and Nate ran out beside her, horror etched on their faces. "The barn—it's on fire!" Claire cried.

Without hesitation, they sprinted toward the flames. The fire spread quickly, the acrid smoke stinging their eyes. Sophie grabbed a nearby fire extinguisher, while Nate ran to call for help.

As they battled the flames, Sophie's anger boiled over. This was Angela's doing—she was sure of it. The fire was meant to send a message, a last, desperate attempt to intimidate them into silence.

But, as they fought to contain the flames, Sophie's resolve only hardened. Angela could threaten, sabotage, and try to scare them off, but they weren't backing down.

After what felt like hours, they finally extinguished the fire, though the barn had suffered extensive damage. Sophie wiped soot from her face, exchanging a weary look with Claire.

"We're not stopping," Sophie said, her voice steady despite her exhaustion. "Angela thinks she can scare us into silence, but she's wrong. We'll see this through to the end."

Claire nodded, her face resolute. "For Uncle James. And for everything he believed in."

Nate joined them, his expression fierce. "Tomorrow, we

take this to the town council. We'll expose Angela's actions, and we'll have the community behind us."

As they stood together in the smoky twilight, Sophie felt a profound sense of unity and purpose. They'd faced Angela's worst, and they were still standing. Tomorrow, they would confront her in front of the entire town, and finally, she would be held accountable.

CHAPTER 18

CRUSHED VINES

THE MORNING DAWNED OVERCAST, the gray sky seeming to reflect the gravity of the day. Sophie, Claire, and Nate gathered at the guesthouse, all exhausted from the fire and tense with anticipation. After last night's sabotage, Sophie knew they had no choice but to press forward. Today, the entire town would learn the truth about Angela's manipulation.

As they reviewed the documents one last time, Nate placed a reassuring hand on Sophie's shoulder. "We're almost there. By tonight, everyone in Sonoma will know what she's done."

Sophie nodded, her heart pounding. She had pieced together Angela's web of manipulation—the financial and emotional pressure she'd placed on James, her control over Claire, and her threats to the community. But, the final piece, she realized, lay with the one person who knew Angela's secrets better than anyone else: Peter Lawton.

"Before the council meeting," Sophie said, her voice steady, "we need to confront Peter. He's been Angela's right hand, and if anyone has information that could seal the case, it's him."

Claire's eyes widened. "Do you think he'll talk to us? He's been loyal to Angela for years."

Sophie paused, considering this. "Maybe. Last night's fire might have shaken him. If we can get him to see the damage Angela's caused—how far she's willing to go—he might realize he's on the wrong side of this."

Nate nodded in agreement. "Peter's always looked out for his own interests. If he sees that siding with Angela could ruin him, he might decide to save himself."

LATER THAT MORNING, Sophie and Nate drove to Peter's office, a modest building on the edge of town. Her nerves hummed as they parked, but her resolve held. This was their last chance to sway Peter before the council meeting.

They found him at his desk, looking unusually tense as he sorted paperwork. He glanced up as they entered, surprise flickering across his face.

"Sophie. Nate. I wasn't expecting company," he said, his voice guarded.

Sophie gave him a calm, steady look. "We need to talk, Peter. About Angela."

Peter's posture stiffened, his expression darkening. "I don't know what you're talking about."

"Oh, I think you do," Sophie replied, holding up a folder of the evidence they'd gathered. "We know about the blackmail, the financial pressure on James, and your threats to Claire. We have enough proof to expose Angela's entire scheme."

Peter's face paled, and for the first time, Sophie saw fear in his eyes. "I—I was just following orders. Angela made it clear I didn't have a choice."

"There's always a choice, Peter," Nate said, his voice firm. "Right now, you can make the right one. If you cooperate, we can help you. But, if you continue supporting Angela, you'll go down with her."

Peter looked away, his gaze darting to the door. Sophie watched as the loyalty he'd maintained for years clashed with the mounting fear of exposure.

"What... what do you want me to do?" he asked finally, his voice barely above a whisper.

Sophie's heart leapt. "We need you to testify at the council meeting this afternoon. Tell the town what you know. If you reveal Angela's manipulation and threats, it'll be enough to end her control for good."

Peter rubbed a hand over his face, his shoulders slumping. "She'll ruin me if I do this."

"She's already tried to ruin us," Nate said, a spark of anger in his tone. "Last night, she set fire to the Cartwright barn. She'll do anything to silence us. Don't you see, Peter? She doesn't care about you—she's only using you."

Peter swallowed, his expression flickering with doubt. Finally, he gave a small nod. "Fine. I'll testify. But, you have to promise I won't be the only one standing against her."

Sophie nodded. "You're not alone, Peter. We're all in this together."

LEAVING PETER'S OFFICE, Sophie felt a renewed sense of purpose. They had everything they needed: the documents, Claire's testimony, and now, Peter's reluctant support. It was time to bring their findings to the town council and reveal Angela's true nature to everyone in Sonoma.

The town hall was already buzzing when they arrived. News of the fire at Cartwright Vineyard had spread quickly, and people gathered in clusters, whispering and casting anxious glances as Sophie, Claire, and Nate entered.

Claire looked around, visibly nervous. "What if they don't believe us, Sophie? Angela's influence runs so deep."

Sophie gave her a reassuring smile, though her own mind churned. She'd seen people like Angela before— people who wielded power like a shield. "They'll believe us," she said. "We have the truth on our side. Once we show them the evidence, Angela won't be able to deny it."

Just as they approached the chamber, Angela appeared in the doorway, flanked by two of her supporters. She locked eyes with Sophie, her gaze filled with fury.

"So, you've really gone this far," she sneered. "I thought you were smarter than this, Sophie."

Sophie held her ground, her voice unwavering. "I'm just doing what's right. Your days of controlling this town are over."

Angela's mouth tightened, but she quickly composed herself, giving Sophie a thin smile. "We'll see about that."

With one last glare, Angela turned and swept into the chamber, her entourage trailing behind her. Sophie watched her go, a surge of determination strengthening her resolve. Angela might be powerful, but this time, the Cartwrights had the truth on their side.

THE COUNCIL CHAMBER WAS PACKED, the tension palpable. The council members took their seats, and the crowd fell silent, all eyes on the front.

Sophie stood beside Claire, Nate, and Peter as the council chairperson opened the floor for public comments. Taking a steadying breath, Sophie stepped forward, holding the folder tightly.

"Thank you for allowing me to speak," she began, her voice strong and clear. "I'm here to present evidence of a coordinated campaign of manipulation, blackmail, and coercion orchestrated by Angela Mason."

A ripple of murmurs spread through the crowd, Angela's supporters exchanging nervous glances. Angela remained outwardly calm, but Sophie noticed a flicker of tension in her gaze.

Holding up the first document, Sophie continued, "These letters and financial records link Angela to a calculated effort to undermine Cartwright Vineyard, pressuring James Cartwright to sell his family's land. She's used threats and blackmail to manipulate the Cartwrights and other members of this community."

The murmurs grew louder as Sophie presented each piece of evidence, detailing Angela's threats to Claire, her coercion of Peter, and her isolation tactics against James. She watched as the council members leaned in, their faces showing growing unease.

Claire stepped forward, her voice trembling but resolute. She spoke about Angela's threats and coercion, how Angela had exploited her loyalty to the Cartwrights to get what she wanted.

"I was afraid," Claire admitted, her voice breaking slightly. "I was afraid of what Angela might do if I didn't cooperate. But, I won't stay silent anymore."

A wave of empathy rippled through the crowd. Several council members nodded, showing a glimmer of understanding. Angela's expression remained stoic, but Sophie saw the tightening in her jaw.

Finally, Peter took the stand, his face pale. "I've served Angela Mason for years, but I can no longer ignore what she's done. She's threatened, manipulated, and damaged lives in this community for her own gain. And I was complicit. Today, I'm here to set the record straight."

As he detailed his involvement and Angela's actions, the room buzzed with shock and anger.

Angela sprang to her feet, her face twisted with fury. "This is all lies!" she spat. "They're conspiring to ruin me!"

Sophie stepped forward, her voice calm yet resolute. "The evidence speaks for itself, Angela. You've spent years using fear and intimidation. But now, the town sees the truth."

The council chairperson raised a hand, calling for order. After a pause, he spoke, his voice steady. "Given the evidence presented today, I believe an investigation is warranted. Angela Mason, we will be reviewing these documents thoroughly. You will be held accountable."

Applause erupted across the room. Sophie exchanged a triumphant look with Claire and Nate. The tide had finally turned.

Angela, her face a mask of rage, pushed through the

crowd and stormed out of the chamber. Sophie watched her go, knowing her hold over the town was broken.

OUTSIDE THE TOWN HALL, Sophie, Claire, and Nate stood together, their relief mingling with a deep sense of accomplishment.

"We did it," Claire whispered, awe in her voice. "We actually did it."

Sophie smiled, feeling the weight of the past few weeks lift. "It was a team effort. And now, Cartwright Vineyard is safe."

Nate placed a hand on Sophie's shoulder, his eyes filled with admiration. "You didn't just solve a mystery, Sophie —you helped this town find its courage."

A warm glow filled Sophie's chest. For the first time since arriving in Sonoma, she felt truly at home. They walked back toward the vineyard, ready to rebuild, united by hope and purpose. Whatever lay ahead, they would face it together.

CHAPTER 19
THE LAST PRESS

THE VICTORY at the town council meeting left Sophie exhilarated, but she knew her work wasn't done. Angela's influence had been exposed, but one piece of the puzzle still nagged at her: James's death. Officially ruled an accident, the details still felt wrong. Angela's web of deceit stretched back years—could she have orchestrated his death?

Sophie spent the morning pouring over the documents once more, replaying the details of his death in her mind. James had been found in the vineyard, with signs suggesting he'd simply tripped and fallen. But, what if that was exactly what Angela wanted everyone to believe?

Claire joined her in the guesthouse, bringing tea and a concerned expression. "Sophie, I can't stop thinking about James. The way he died... it doesn't feel right. He was so careful, always steady on his feet."

Sophie's thoughts returned to the night James was found. Claire's voice echoed in her mind: *"He tripped and fell, but it doesn't feel right."* The image of James, steady and meticulous, clashed with the explanation.

She reviewed the coroner's report again. There it was—traces of a sedative. Sophie's stomach turned. "Angela didn't just push him to sell," she whispered. "She ensured he wouldn't get the chance."

Sophie nodded, her suspicions growing. "Angela's manipulation runs deeper than we realized. If she feared James might sell to someone else, or if he was planning to hold his ground... she might have taken drastic action."

The memory of the funeral flashed in Sophie's mind. The entire town had gathered to honor James, their respect evident in every bowed head. Sophie had stood beside Claire, anger and grief mixing as she promised herself she'd uncover the truth.

Claire's face grew pale, but she nodded resolutely. "What do you need me to do? I want to find the truth."

Sophie felt a surge of gratitude for Claire's support. They were in this together, determined to uncover every last secret.

As they sifted through the final stack of documents, Sophie noticed something unusual—a crumpled scrap of paper stuck between two folders. She carefully unfolded it, revealing a scribbled note in James's handwriting. It read:

"Angela's offers keep increasing. Something feels wrong. Must find out what Peter's been up to."

Sophie's pulse quickened. This was the clue she'd been looking for. James hadn't trusted Angela's persistent offers, and it seemed he'd been on the verge of discovering something significant.

"What does it mean?" Claire asked, peering over her shoulder.

Sophie studied the note. "James must have suspected that Angela and Peter were collaborating on something beyond a buyout. He might have been planning to confront Peter directly."

As they continued searching, Sophie's eye caught another document—a signed check from James to a construction contractor for a substantial sum, dated just before his death. Yet, according to Claire, no construction had been done recently.

"Claire, was James planning any work on the vineyard before he died?" Sophie asked, holding up the check.

Claire shook her head. "Not that he mentioned. But, he did say something about 'safety improvements' weeks before he passed. I assumed it was routine maintenance."

Sophie's eyes narrowed. "What if he uncovered something dangerous—something that wasn't accidental?"

A sinking feeling spread through her. Angela and Peter had been willing to go to great lengths to secure control of the vineyard. If James had uncovered a deliberate safety hazard they'd introduced, it could explain his need to confront Peter.

"This isn't just about blackmail," Sophie said, urgency creeping into her voice. "James might have discovered something that put him in real danger—and Angela used it to push him out."

SOPHIE AND CLAIRE rushed to Peter's office, hoping to find the missing piece of evidence. After the council meeting, Peter had reluctantly agreed to let them review his records, but he'd been evasive, as though he still had something to hide.

Peter looked up from his desk as they entered, his face pale. "I thought we were done with this," he said, his voice tight.

"Peter," Sophie began, her tone unyielding, "we need to know if you and Angela had anything to do with James's death. We found a check for construction work that was never done. I think James discovered something, and Angela had a hand in silencing him."

Peter's face crumpled, his gaze falling to the desk. "You don't understand... Angela... she's more ruthless than you know. I was just trying to protect myself."

"Protect yourself?" Claire's voice was filled with disbelief and hurt. "James trusted you, and you helped Angela push him out of his own vineyard!"

Peter's hands shook as he raked them through his hair. "I never wanted anyone hurt. Angela... she threatened me, too. Said she'd ruin me if I didn't follow along. I didn't know she'd go this far."

Sophie leaned forward, her gaze unyielding. "Tell us the truth, Peter. Did Angela have anything to do with James's death?"

After a long pause, Peter nodded slowly, his voice a broken whisper. "Angela instructed me to arrange 'safety adjustments' around the vineyard. She said it was just to encourage James to sell, to make it feel like the place was too much to manage. But, I never thought it would turn deadly."

Peter reached into his desk drawer and pulled out a worn, faded letter. "Here," he said. "Angela's instructions. She had me contact the contractor to 'adjust' parts of the vineyard pathways. She called it a 'nudge,' but I should have known better."

Sophie read the letter again, her hands trembling. Angela's calculated words detailed a chilling plan to force James into selling. The letter included specifics: hiring contractors to sabotage the vineyard's pathways, disguising it as routine maintenance, and ensuring James felt pressured to sell before financial ruin.

"This isn't just blackmail," Sophie said, her voice shaking. "This is premeditated. She didn't care who she hurt, as long as she got what she wanted."

"But it's enough," Nate added. "This is the proof the council needs to take her down."

BACK AT THE VINEYARD, Sophie, Claire, and Nate reviewed the evidence one last time. The letter from Angela, the unused construction check, and Peter's confession painted a damning picture. Angela had manipulated every detail to push James into selling, and when her plan failed, it had ultimately led to his death.

Sophie looked at Claire, her gaze steady. "This is what we'll bring to the town tomorrow. We'll reveal Angela's role in James's death and expose her for what she is. She won't escape this."

Claire's face softened with gratitude, though sadness lingered in her eyes. "Thank you, Sophie. I don't know how I'd have done this without you. Uncle James deserves justice, and now he'll finally have it."

Nate put a comforting arm around Claire. "Tomorrow, we'll stand together. When the town hears this, Angela won't have a single ally left."

As they shared a moment of solidarity, Sophie felt a quiet sense of closure. This investigation had been more than solving a mystery. It was a journey of healing, justice, and finding purpose. Sonoma was no longer just a temporary stop; it had become a home.

But, there was still one ultimate act: confronting Angela before the entire town.

THAT NIGHT, Sophie sat at her laptop, her thoughts flowing as she typed her latest Substack post. The words came easily, capturing the weight of everything they'd uncovered.

> "When I first arrived in Sonoma, I didn't know what I was looking for. I came seeking peace, a fresh start, and maybe a chance to rebuild. But I found something far deeper—a town worth fighting for, people who welcomed me as one of their own, and a truth that needed light.
>
> Angela Mason built her power on fear, turning people's secrets and doubts into weapons. She wielded that power ruthlessly, but her influence ends here. Tomorrow, the truth will come out.
>
> Sometimes, justice isn't just about punishing the guilty. It's about honoring those who stood by their

convictions, who fought for what was right even when it wasn't easy. And with the support of Sonoma, I know we'll see this through to the end."

She hit "publish" and sat back, feeling a wave of calm. This post wasn't just for her readers—it was a testament to everything she'd endured, a promise to herself to always stand up for what was right, and a tribute to James's legacy.

THE NEXT MORNING, Sophie and her friends gathered the evidence, preparing for the final confrontation. She looked at Claire and Nate, feeling a rush of gratitude and purpose.

"Let's end this," Sophie said, her voice steady. "For James. For the vineyard. And for everyone who's stood by us."

Together, they left the guesthouse, ready to face whatever the day might bring.

CHAPTER 20
A VINTAGE REVELATION

THE AIR WAS CHARGED with anticipation as the crowd filled the Sonoma town hall. Rumors of Angela's schemes, her grip over the vineyard, and whispers of her involvement in James's death had spread like wildfire. Faces in the crowd reflected curiosity, skepticism, and the faint hope that justice would finally be served.

Sophie stood at the front, flanked by Claire, Nate, and Peter. She felt the weight of the town's expectations on her shoulders, but her resolve was unbreakable. Today, Sonoma would finally know the truth.

At exactly noon, the town council members took their seats, and the crowd quieted. The council chair, a dignified woman with silver hair named Joan Callahan, looked out over the assembly, then nodded at Sophie.

"Sophie Brooks, you've requested to address the council and the community. The floor is yours."

Sophie stepped forward, clutching the folder of evidence. She took a deep breath, steadying herself before she spoke.

"Thank you, Joan. And thank you all for being here today." Sophie's voice was clear and calm as she looked out over the audience. "I came to Sonoma seeking peace and a fresh start. What I found was a community overshadowed by one person's relentless pursuit of control—Angela Mason."

A murmur rippled through the crowd, and Sophie caught sight of Angela seated near the back, her face a mask of indifference. But, Sophie could see the tension in her posture, the way her eyes narrowed with thinly veiled fury.

"Angela has spent years manipulating this town," Sophie continued, holding up the folder. "She used intimidation, financial pressure, and even blackmail to control those around her. She tried to seize the Cartwright Vineyard by any means necessary, undermining James Cartwright's legacy and isolating him from his family and friends."

Sophie opened the folder and held up the first piece of evidence—a letter from Angela to Peter, detailing her plans to pressure James into selling.

"This letter shows Angela's intent to manipulate James into selling his land. She encouraged unsafe conditions at the vineyard, hoping he'd feel overwhelmed and give up. When that didn't work, she escalated, pressuring his niece, Claire, through blackmail."

Claire stepped forward, her voice trembling but resolute as she addressed the crowd. "Angela threatened me, using my loyalty to my family against me. She told me that if I didn't cooperate, she'd destroy our reputation and make it impossible for us to keep the vineyard. I was afraid. But, I won't stay silent anymore."

The crowd gasped, shocked whispers filling the room as they absorbed Claire's words. Joan Callahan motioned for silence, her expression somber as she turned back to Sophie. "Do you have further evidence, Ms. Brooks?"

Sophie nodded, holding up the last letter they'd uncovered—the damning piece tying Angela to James's death.

"This letter from Angela to Peter shows she instructed him to make 'modifications' to the vineyard pathways. She called it a 'subtle nudge,' but these so-called modifications led to the very conditions that caused James Cartwright's accident. This was no accident—it was a calculated risk on Angela's part, one that ultimately cost James his life."

A heavy silence filled the room. Shock and outrage were clear on the faces of the townspeople, many of whom had once counted themselves among Angela's supporters. Even the council members looked shaken, their gaze shifting between Sophie and Angela, who had now risen from her seat, her face a mask of fury.

"This is absurd!" Angela's voice cut through the silence, sharp and venomous. "You have no proof that I had anything to do with James's death. This is a witch hunt, orchestrated by a meddling outsider who doesn't understand our town!"

Before she could continue, Peter stepped forward, his face pale but resolute.

"I was complicit in Angela's schemes," he said, loud enough for all to hear. "I arranged for the 'modifications' at her request, believing her claims that it was just to make James more open to selling. I convinced myself it was harmless, but now... now I see the consequences. And, I can't stay silent any longer."

Angela shot Peter a look of pure loathing, but he held

his ground. "Angela Mason manipulated this town for her own gain, and I was a part of it. But, the truth has to come out."

The crowd erupted, anger and disbelief rippling through the room. People who had once admired Angela now looked at her with horror and betrayal.

Joan Callahan called for order, her voice firm as she turned to Angela. "Ms. Mason, do you have anything to say in your defense?"

Angela's face contorted with fury. "This is all lies! A ridiculous story spun by people who have always resented my success. None of this proves anything!"

Sophie stepped forward, meeting Angela's gaze with unflinching determination. "You can deny it all you want, Angela, but the town sees you for who you are now. You've controlled people through fear, but that ends today."

Angela's mask cracked, and for the first time, Sophie saw genuine fear flicker in her eyes. She knew that her hold over the town was slipping. In one last act of defiance, she turned on her heel and stormed out of the town hall, her footsteps echoing in the stunned silence.

As the townspeople dispersed, Sophie felt a wave of exhaustion wash over her. The weight of the past few weeks finally lifted. She looked at Claire and Nate, her heart swelling with pride and gratitude.

"We did it," Claire whispered, her eyes filling with tears. "James can finally rest in peace."

Nate placed a comforting arm around her shoulders.

"The vineyard is safe, and Angela won't be able to hurt anyone here again."

As they walked out of the town hall, Sophie felt a deep sense of satisfaction. She had come to Sonoma to find herself, but she had also found a family, a community worth fighting for, and a purpose beyond her own life.

Outside, the sheriff approached, a solemn expression on his face. "Thank you, Sophie," he said, his tone genuine. "You exposed something that's been festering here for years. Angela Mason will face justice, and this town is stronger because of you."

Sophie nodded, her relief palpable. "Thank you, Sheriff. I only wanted to do what was right—for James, and for everyone here."

He gave her a respectful nod. "You did more than that. You helped this town find its courage again."

As the sheriff walked away, Sophie felt a profound sense of closure. Angela's reign was over, and the Cartwright Vineyard was finally safe.

THAT NIGHT, Nate invited Sophie and Claire to his restaurant for a quiet celebration. The small gathering was filled with laughter, relief, and a deep sense of camaraderie. They toasted to James's memory, the vineyard's future, and the community they'd fought to protect.

As the evening wound down, Nate pulled Sophie aside, his expression warm. "You know, Sophie, Sonoma's lucky to have you," he said. "You've done something incredible here."

Sophie felt a blush rise to her cheeks. "I couldn't have

done it without you. You reminded me what it means to stand up for something worth fighting for."

They shared a quiet moment, their unspoken connection deepening. Sophie felt a warmth she hadn't allowed herself to feel in years. For the first time, she was at peace —and she knew that this place, this community, was home.

"Stay in Sonoma," Nate said, his gaze unwavering. "We need people like you here."

Sophie's heart swelled with gratitude, and she nodded, a soft smile spreading across her face. "I think I might."

As they rejoined Claire and the others, Sophie felt a sense of belonging and purpose. She'd come to Sonoma seeking a fresh start, and she'd found it—along with a family, a cause, and a place to call home.

CHAPTER 21
THE FRUITS OF FRIENDSHIP

THE MORNING AFTER THE CONFRONTATION, a peaceful stillness settled over Cartwright Vineyard. The weight of the past few weeks had lifted, leaving behind a comforting quiet. Sophie woke early, feeling lighter than she had since arriving in Sonoma. As she looked out at the rows of vines stretching toward the sunrise, she felt a connection to this place that surprised her—more like home than any place she'd been in years.

As she walked to the main house, she found Claire sitting on the porch, cradling a steaming mug of tea. Claire looked up with a soft smile, and Sophie joined her, sinking into the chair beside her.

"Feels different, doesn't it?" Claire said, gazing over the vineyard. "Like we're finally free."

Sophie nodded, pride swelling as she looked at her friend. Claire had endured so much, yet she'd emerged stronger, her spirit unbroken. "It's like a weight's been lifted from the whole town. People don't have to live in Angela's shadow anymore."

They sat in comfortable silence for a moment, watching the sunlight cast golden rays over the vines, making them shimmer with a kind of quiet resilience.

"I keep thinking about James," Claire said, her voice thick with emotion. "He poured everything into this vineyard. It's because of him we have something worth fighting for."

Sophie placed a comforting hand on her shoulder. "James would be so proud of you, Claire. You fought for his legacy, for everything he believed in. You never backed down, even when things got rough."

Claire looked down, a bittersweet smile on her face. "Sometimes, I wanted to give up. When Angela's threats felt overwhelming. But then... I thought of what this vineyard means to my family, to this town. I knew I couldn't let her take it."

Sophie felt a surge of empathy. She knew the struggle to keep going in the face of adversity, to find strength when it felt impossible. "You did more than just keep going, Claire. You inspired everyone around you. You're stronger than you realize."

Claire's eyes glistened as she looked at Sophie. "I couldn't have done it without you, Sophie. You came here and saw what no one else did. You believed in me and in this place. I'll never forget that."

Sophie smiled, moved by her friend's words.

"You've given me just as much, Claire," Sophie said. "You gave me a place in something meaningful. Friendship, family, a real home."

They shared a quiet moment, a sense of closure settling between them. They'd fought hard for this vineyard, for James's legacy, and for each other. As the sun rose over the vineyard, they knew a bright future lay ahead.

LATER THAT DAY, Sophie and Claire hosted a small gathering at the vineyard to celebrate its future. They invited close friends and community members who had stood by them. Nate was there, along with several vineyard workers, some of Claire's family and friends, and even Sheriff Davis, who surprised everyone with a rare but genuine smile.

The afternoon sunlight warmed the gathering, laughter and conversation filling the air. Alive and vibrant, the vineyard was filled with the sense of renewal that had enveloped the town. The tension that Angela's presence had cast seemed to have dissolved, replaced by unity and resilience.

Nate approached Sophie as she watched the gathering from a distance, a glass of wine in hand. He gave her a warm smile. "I've been meaning to thank you, you know. You didn't just solve a mystery—you reminded us all of what this town stands for."

Sophie felt a blush rise to her cheeks, but she smiled. "I couldn't have done it without you and Claire. This place, these people... you've all made Sonoma feel like home."

Nate's expression softened, his eyes lingering on her face. "You belong here, Sophie. I think Sonoma has been waiting for someone like you for a long time."

Sophie's heart warmed at his words, a deep sense of certainty settling within her. She'd found what she was searching for—a place she could truly belong. Yet, a flicker of doubt crept in. Belonging wasn't just about where you were; it was about who you were. She had spent years running from herself, from the choices that had brought her here.

"I love this place," Sophie said softly, her voice almost lost in the rustling leaves. "But before I can stay, I need to know that I can stand on my own. Otherwise, I'll never be able to fully embrace it."

Nate studied her, his gaze understanding. "You're not running anymore. You're finding your way. And when you're ready, you'll know where home is."

As the gathering wound down, Claire suggested a walk through the vineyard. They strolled together along the rows of vines, their footsteps soft on the sun-warmed earth. The vines were bearing the early buds of the new season, symbols of hope and renewal.

"This place is beautiful," Sophie said, her voice filled with awe. "I can see why James loved it so much."

Claire nodded, a bittersweet smile on her face. "It's more than just land. It's history, family, community. And now, it's part of our future."

They paused near an old oak tree, one James had told her was planted by his great-grandfather. Claire touched its rough bark, her gaze distant. "I used to come here with him. He'd tell me stories about the vineyard, about our family's history. He always said that each vine was a testament to the people who'd come before us."

Sophie placed a hand on Claire's shoulder, her heart

swelling. "James would be so proud of you, Claire. You've honored his memory in the best way possible."

Claire took a deep breath, her eyes shining with emotion. "Thank you, Sophie. For everything."

They stood under the oak tree for a quiet moment, the weight of their journey giving way to a deep sense of peace. They had honored James's legacy, and now, together, they would carry it forward.

THAT EVENING, after the guests had left, and the vineyard had returned to its serene quiet, Sophie sat on the porch of her guesthouse, reflecting on the whirlwind of events that had brought her to this moment. She opened her laptop and began a new post for her Substack, capturing everything she'd learned and experienced.

"When I first came to Sonoma, I was looking for a fresh start, a place to heal. I never expected to find myself in the middle of a mystery that would change my life forever.

This journey has been filled with twists and turns, challenges I never saw coming, and people who've shown me the true meaning of friendship and community. Together, we stood up to someone who cast a shadow over this town, and we reclaimed something that belongs to all of us—a sense of hope, unity, and belonging.

James Cartwright once said that a vineyard is more than just land. It's a legacy, a testament to the people who came before us, and a promise to those who will come after. As I look out over these vines, I feel that legacy and that promise, and I know I'm exactly where I'm meant to be."

She paused, a profound sense of fulfillment washing over her. She'd arrived in Sonoma as an outsider, but now she was part of something far bigger than herself. This place, these people—they were her family.

With a smile, she hit "publish," feeling the satisfying closure of a chapter well-written.

As she closed her laptop, Sophie felt a sense of excitement for the future. There was still so much to explore, both in Sonoma and beyond. But for now, she was content to live in the moment, and to savor the feeling of belonging she'd found.

Nate appeared at the edge of the porch, his smile warm as he joined her. They sat together in the evening's quiet, watching the last light fade over the vineyard.

"What's next for you, Sophie Brooks?" he asked softly.

Sophie smiled, her gaze drifting over the rows of vines. "I don't know yet. But, I have a feeling it'll be something good."

They shared a quiet laugh, their connection deepening as they sat together in the warm Sonoma night. Sophie knew that whatever the future held, she was ready—because she'd found her place, her purpose, and a family to call her own.

And, for the first time in a long time, she felt truly, undeniably at peace.

CHAPTER 22
ROOTS AND REFLECTIONS

THE EARLY MORNING sun cast a soft, golden glow over Cartwright Vineyard as Sophie strolled along the rows of vines. The familiar scent of damp earth and budding leaves filled the air, and she felt the coolness of the dewy grass underfoot. Each step along the vineyard rows was unhurried, peaceful—a sharp contrast to the whirlwind that had been her life these last few months.

The town had moved on from Angela's reign. Although many still reeled from the shock of her manipulations, there was now a palpable sense of hope. The Cartwright Vineyard was safe, and James's legacy had been restored, a testament to resilience and the community's strength.

Sophie reached the crest of a hill overlooking the vineyard, the same spot where James would stand and survey his land each morning. Closing her eyes, she breathed in deeply, almost as if he were there beside her—his presence woven into the soil, the vines, and the morning sky. In that quiet moment, she felt connected not only to James but to

Sonoma itself. This wasn't just a town; it was a family, a place where she finally felt she belonged.

THAT AFTERNOON, as the sun cast warm rays across the guesthouse porch, Sophie sat with her laptop, ready to write her last post about her time in Sonoma. The words flowed easily, capturing everything she'd learned and the memories she'd made.

> "When I arrived in Sonoma, I was searching for a new beginning, a way to rebuild after heartbreak. I never expected to become part of a mystery that would test me in ways I couldn't have imagined.
>
> But this journey has taught me that true strength often lies in our connections with others—in friendships that shape us, in places that welcome us, and in the legacies we choose to carry forward.
>
> The Cartwright Vineyard isn't just a piece of land. It's a testament to the people who fought for it, to James Cartwright's memory, and to a community that stands united. Together, we faced fear and reclaimed what was ours—a sense of unity, hope, and belonging.
>
> As I look ahead, I'm filled with excitement. There are mysteries yet to unravel, places yet to discover. And wherever I go, I know a part of Sonoma will always be with me."

Sophie hit "publish" and leaned back, feeling a sense of deep satisfaction. This chapter of her life had come to a close, but Sonoma would always remain a part of her. With its warm people, beautiful landscapes, and steadfast resilience, it had changed her forever.

Just as she closed her laptop, her phone buzzed with a text. She glanced at the screen, her heart skipping a beat when she saw the name. Nate.

> Nate: I heard you're leaving tomorrow. I just wanted to say... Sonoma isn't going to be the same without you. Take care, Sophie. Don't forget about us.

Sophie smiled softly, her fingers hovering over the keyboard before typing back.

> Sophie: I could never forget. Sonoma has a way of staying with you. I'll be back someday. Promise.

She set the phone aside, a faint tug at her heart reminding her of everything she was leaving behind. But Sonoma wasn't gone—it was woven into her now, in the friendships she'd made and the lessons she'd learned.

Just as she closed her laptop, her phone buzzed with a text from Oliver.

> Oliver: Read your post. It's beautiful, Soph. You've really found your place, haven't you?

Sophie smiled, her fingers typing quickly.

> Sophie: I have. It's hard to explain, but... Sonoma feels like home.

> Oliver: So what's next? There's an old villa
> in Italy with a few mysteries of its own.
> Think you're up for it?

Sophie's heart fluttered at the thought. Another mystery, another adventure. She glanced out at the vineyard one last time, feeling the tug of excitement mingled with bittersweet fondness.

> Sophie: Italy sounds perfect. Let's do it.

THE NEXT DAY, Claire and Nate joined Sophie at the guesthouse to help her pack. Laughter and conversation filled the air as they boxed up her books, mementos, and the little treasures she'd collected in Sonoma. The guesthouse had been more than just a place to stay—it had become a sanctuary, a place where she'd found herself again.

As they finished packing, Nate turned to her, a teasing smile replacing the bittersweet one she'd seen so often in the past few days. "Don't think you're getting out of harvest season. Sonoma has a way of pulling people back."

Sophie laughed softly, her heart lifting. "I wouldn't miss it for the world." The weight of his earlier message still lingered, but now it felt like an unspoken promise—a bridge back to this place when the time was right.

Claire pulled her into a warm embrace. "Thank you, Sophie. For everything. For fighting for my family, for standing by me. I don't know what I would've done without you."

Sophie hugged her tightly, feeling the weight of their shared journey. "You're strong, Claire. You always were. Sonoma is lucky to have you."

They held each other, and Sophie thought back to the early days—how fragile things had felt, how far they'd come together.

They walked to her car together, lingering in the driveway as she loaded the last of her things. She looked at her friends—her family, really—and felt an overwhelming gratitude. They'd become part of her story, just as she'd become part of theirs.

With one last wave, she started the car and drove away, glancing back to see Claire and Nate framed by the morning light. As they faded into the distance, she felt not sadness, but readiness. She was ready for whatever lay ahead, confident that she'd carry the lessons of Sonoma with her.

As Sophie drove down the winding road out of Sonoma, she felt a familiar excitement stirring within her. The world was vast, filled with mysteries waiting to be solved, each one a new chapter waiting to unfold.

She thought of the villa in Italy—its ancient stones, its hidden stories. She thought of Oliver, always by her side, ready for the next adventure. She'd come to Sonoma searching for herself, and now, having found her strength, she was ready to embrace whatever came next.

With a smile, she turned on the radio, letting the music fill the car as she drove toward the future. The vineyard, the friendships, and the memories she'd made in Sonoma would stay with her, a constant reminder of the power of friendship, courage, and standing up for what's right.

As the road stretched out before her, Sophie Brooks— the writer turned amateur detective—felt alive with possibility.

Her adventure was just beginning.

The End

Did you enjoy *Wine and Whispers*?
Please consider rating or reviewing it on Goodreads, Bookbub or your favorite retailer.

Have you read the FREE prequel? Download *Feasts and Farewells*, Sophie's short origin story.

Read *Olives and Obsessions*, the next book in the **Sophie Brooks Mysteries.**

Join my newsletter to read Sophie's **blog, recipes and wine pairings**!

TheWanderingFork

TheWanderingFork My time in Sonoma has been full of delicious surprises and even a few mysteries 🍸 ✦. Thank you to everyone who followed along! I'll be sharing recipes inspired by my stay (hint: winter greens and goat cheese are involved). Make sure you're subscribed to my newsletter for all the details! #SonomaFarewell #FarmToTableAdventures #WineCountry #TravelAndTaste

ABOUT THE AUTHOR

Daisy Landish is a clean romance and cozy mystery author whose clean and sweet novellas have tugged at readers' heartstrings around the world. When she's not writing love stories, Daisy spends her time reading, hiking at dawn, and riding into the sunset on her horse, Rosebud.

Join Daisy's Newsletter for updates and giveaways!
www.daisylandishromance.com

facebook.com/daisylandishromance

x.com/daisy_landish

instagram.com/daisylandishbooks

amazon.com/author/daisylandish

bookbub.com/authors/daisy-landish

goodreads.com/Daisy_Landish

ALSO BY DAISY LANDISH

Clean Regency Romance

Christmas with the Earl

The Lady Series - The Allington Collection

The Lady Series - The Gillingham Collection

The Lady Series - The Blackmore Collection

The Lady Series - The Norrington Collection

Clean Contemporary Romance

Timeline Retreats

Maplewood Grove Series

Love on Spruce Island

Second Chance

Cherry Tree Island

The Wedding Trio

Extra Credit

Counting on the Cowboy

Focusing on the Cowboy

Mistletoe Magic

Grounded at Christmas

Cozy Mysteries

Lady Ashcoombe Mysteries

Sophie Brooks Mysteries

Jane and Kennedy Daniels Mysteries

Pine Grove Mysteries

Annie Archer Paranormal Mysteries

Wilma Wade Holiday Mysteries

Mike and Maddie Mysteries

Mystic Moonhaven Mysteries

Cozy Mystery Samplers

Sweater Weather: Cozy Mysteries for Fall

Summer Vibes: Cozy Mysteries for Summer

Let it Snow: Cozy Mysteries for Winter

Spring Break: Cozy Mysteries for Spring